By Megan Bryce

The Reluctant Bride Collection

To Catch A Spinster
To Tame A Dragon
To Wed The Widow
To Tempt The Saint

A Temporary Engagement

Some Like It Charming
Some Like It Ruthless
Some Like It Perfect
Some Like It Hopeless

To Catch A Spinster

THE RELUCTANT BRIDE COLLECTION

BOOK ONE

BOOK ONE

MEGAN BRYCE

To Catch A Spinster
The Reluctant Bride Collection,
Book One

ISBN: 0692450297
ISBN-13: 978-0692450291

meganbrycebooks@gmail.com

If you would like to be notified
when a new title becomes
available, sign up at
meganbryce.com

To my husband–
because he makes my life,
and my books,
better.

Prologue

Miss Olivia Blakesley watched as her youngest sister was married and thought, "That does it, old girl. You are officially on the shelf."

Truthfully, she wasn't quite yet. But at the ripe old age of seven and twenty, with two older sisters and three younger sisters all married, she was close enough. What man would want the sister who had been left behind? More importantly, why would she want the man who would want her?

She wouldn't. So it was a good thing she had her studies and responsibilities. She was fairly certain she would have gone stark raving mad these last eight years waiting for a suitor who would never come if she hadn't started studying the stars or helping her father with the accounts. Not exactly respectable activities for a gentle young woman, but she enjoyed them.

Her mother blamed those activities for her current matrimonial-less state. What woman would rather sneak outside to paint stars than flirt with a beau? What woman who was at least pretending she wanted to get married would wear those high-necked, front-buttoned, somber-colored old maid rags?

Olivia handed her mother, who sat sniffling in the pew beside her, a clean handkerchief.

"Thank you, Olivia. I can always count on your handkerchief to be dry at weddings, can't I? I don't understand how you can be so emotionless."

"I'm not emotionless, and you should be grateful as you now have two handkerchiefs to drench."

Olivia's father winked at her as he patted his wife's hand. "It's not as if this wedding was a surprise, my dear."

No, Eugenia had been promising that she would be snatched up the quickest since Prudence had taken nearly two years in the marriage mart. Eugenia had lasted a mere two months. The Blakesley sisters were nothing if not goal-oriented.

Olivia had her own goals and, unfortunately for her mother, they did not include catching a husband. Even so, she did not want to die inexperienced in love, estranged from her sisters because they knew something she didn't.

Lust.

She did not want to die a virgin spinster aunt, caring for her aging parents.

It would be much better if she could die an *experienced* spinster aunt, caring for her aging parents.

She glanced at the cross hanging above the vicar's head. Dear Lord, what was she considering? Was she really thinking of. . .

No. It was a sin. And she was in a church, for heaven's sake.

But as her father was wont to say: In the course of life, some commandments must be broken. For emergencies. For science.

Thou shalt not kill. Definitely one to be broken in an emergency.

Thou shalt not worship any graven images. A few might say that Olivia worshiped her Dutch-made telescope. For science, of course.

Honor thy father and mother. She had never been any good at that one.

Thou shalt not commit adultery. . .

Well, she just wouldn't choose a married man. This was, after all, a scientific emergency. She was not going to die an old maid.

Olivia looked back at the altar. Her beautiful sister in her lace-trimmed ivory satin wedding gown beamed at her new husband, who looked down at her with obvious love and a little bit of panic. Olivia would never have that. She would never fall in love. Never have someone to depend on– only herself.

She nodded. So be it. If she could not have everything, she would have something. If she could not have love, she would have lust. She would find someone to teach her desire.

Amen.

One

Mr. Nathaniel Jenkins had never wanted to dunk himself in the punch bowl and drown himself more than he did at that moment. The young lady before him was slowly turning his brain to mush and he was afraid it would start dribbling out his ears at any moment.

"And then I told the seamstress I wanted six ruffles. Three on the bodice and three on the hem."

Of course, if it gave him an excuse to leave he wouldn't mind a little dribbling. He glanced at his mother, who wasn't even trying to hide her scowl, and decided not even that could get him out of this evening.

Nathaniel sighed into his glass. What he needed was something a little stronger than punch.

He took a small sip and sighed again. What he really needed was a mother who left him alone. The woman had four grandchildren already, wasn't that enough?

If her expression was anything to go by, no.

"I had to pay nearly double. Outrageous." The young lady fingered a ruffle on her bodice and smiled coyly. "But it was worth it, don't you think?"

She looked like she would fly away in a stiff breeze but Nathaniel nodded. "You look quite. . . lovely."

Her next dance partner came to relieve him and Nathaniel downed the rest of his punch in relief. He had done his duty, now he might be able to make his escape.

His mother slipped up beside

him. "Nathaniel, really. You were quite rude, you hardly said a word to Miss Mayes."

"I could hardly get a word in, Mother. She did allow me to compliment her, though."

"Hmmph. Can you not try to like these girls? You need a wife, Nathaniel. You are the head of this family now and you need an heir."

"I already have one. Diana's son is my heir."

"No matter how much we love Matthew, a nephew is not an acceptable heir. I do not understand how you can be so thick-headed about this."

He knew his duty. Marry a young girl from a respectable family and father an heir. But he could not find it in himself to marry any of these empty-headed, brightly-colored chatterboxes. They looked like they should still be in the nursery. As for bedding one? Unless he could glue their mouths shut, it seemed impossible.

Perhaps he was too old. At thirty-nine, an eighteen- year-old girl seemed as foreign as a sunny day in February.

Or perhaps he was too young. In another ten years he might jump at the chance to marry a young chit with her hair in braids. All he knew was he couldn't do it now.

And if all he was being offered were these girls, he would not be getting married.

"Mother, if you really have a desire to see me married, I would suggest finding girls a little older. And quieter. And not so. . . frilly."

"You are a bigger stick-in-the-mud than your father."

"It is the custom nowadays for new heirs to outdo their father in some way. How gratifying to know I've achieved it."

She tapped his arm lightly with her fan. "Perhaps I could ask your sister to look around."

Nathaniel groaned. "Diana pops around with her unsuspecting

friends enough as it is."

"I doubt her friends are quite as unsuspecting as you think. You're quite the catch, if I do say so myself."

"Just what a man wants to hear from his mother."

She nodded decisively. "It's true, nonetheless. You have a stable fortune, good relations, and, if not a title, then land."

"I feel like a prize stallion."

"Don't be so melodramatic, dear. Even the lowliest stable-boy will find a mate. So should you."

His gaze slid slowly over the crowd. "It seems that a lowly stable-boy would have more choice than I."

His mother waved her hand impatiently. "There are as many different girls as there are fish in the sea."

"They seem to be all the same species to me, Mother."

"Hmm. Well, we'll just have to find one that's a little different."

Nathaniel watched her inspect the girls nearest to her and bit back a laugh. "Good luck to you. Until then I'll be at my club."

Mrs. Anne Jenkins smiled up at her son, slipping her arm through his. "I don't think you'll find any suitable girls at your club. Besides, you agreed to take me home tonight. I see you so little as it is."

"This would be so much easier if you would just arrange it all for me."

"I would, dear, if you'd let me. But you have so many requirements for a wife."

"I have three: not young, not chatty, not frilly. It's not as if I'm being uncooperative."

Mrs. Jenkins looked at the sea of young, chatty, frilly girls and patted his arm. "Well, I'm sure I'll find someone for you." She let out a long breath. "Hopefully."

Olivia had been studying the men at the ball since she arrived. Since her sister's wedding she had done nothing but imagine the perfect seducer. Tall, but not too tall. Handsome, but not diabolically so. Experienced, but not a rake. Good Lord, definitely not a rake. She did have a reputation to preserve. To be seen with a libertine would embarrass herself and her family.

Also, one of her brothers-in-law was a reformed rake. It was possible he knew more about the sexual arts than the others, but that sister was always worried that she would not be enough to, ahem, satisfy him.

Olivia had taken to listening at doors in her younger days.

But she had learned a good many things that way, and when no one would talk to you about certain subjects, it really was the only way.

So, no rake for her. She would like a gentle introduction, not a dunk in a cold pond.

He would need to be a gentle man, but not that gentle since he would have to seduce her. Obviously, not married. And above all, the very most important trait he would need to possess would be discretion. He could not tell anyone. Ever.

The list she'd made for a husband had not been this long.

It really was no wonder she hadn't found anyone yet. She'd been searching for a husband eight years and that task was beginning to sound like a walk in the park compared to this.

The only gentleman she hadn't dismissed outright was the one in the corner who looked like he wanted to poke his eyes out. She'd spoken to his companion a few times herself and understood the feeling. That unfortunate shade of orange didn't help the girl either.

But while Miss Mayes might look supremely silly, he looked quite responsible. Mature. Stoic in the face of adversity.

Tight-lipped.

He did not look the sort to tell tales at all.

He did look a bit tall but she supposed lying down it wouldn't matter. His dark brown hair was a bit longer than fashion dictated but as it was slightly curly, she approved. Her own stick-straight hair refused to curl, even with tongs.

His form was pleasing. Firm thighs, wide shoulders. Quite manly, actually.

Hmm.

Olivia leaned toward her younger sister, Mary. Not only was she Olivia's closest sister, but she also had a knack for knowing interesting tidbits about nearly everyone.

"Do you know who the gentleman in the far corner is?"

Mary looked discreetly. "Mr. Nathaniel Jenkins, the only son of Mrs. Anne Jenkins. Her husband died almost two years ago and Mr. Jenkins has still not taken a bride."

"If she insists on him talking to silly young girls with too many flounces, it's no wonder. I would like to be introduced to him."

"Olivia, really!"

"Could you find your husband, Mary?"

"You are being quite forward."

Olivia sipped her punch. Yes, indeed she was. The season was nearly half over and this was her last one– no matter what her mother said.

Olivia said, "Time is running out."

"Oh, well, yes. I see what you mean. I'll go find him."

Olivia smiled slightly. "Thank you. That would be most helpful."

Olivia watched as Mary wound her way to Rufus. He smiled at his wife and for once in her life Olivia envied one of her sisters. With his quick charm, ready laughter, and silly pranks, Rufus was her favorite brother-in-law. He was rarely serious and had been in love with Mary for longer than anyone could remember. They were a good match, but then they'd lived next door to each other since birth. They'd been married at eighteen.

If Olivia could have chosen her fate, that would have been it. Best friend and lover, rolled into one.

Rufus looked in surprise at Olivia, then winked.

She sighed and shook her head. Of course, she much preferred Rufus as a brother-in-law than as a husband. She'd be much too tempted to smack him if he was her husband.

Nathaniel nodded as Rufus Eliot hailed him. Though Eliot was part of the younger set, they were acquainted through their club. A likable enough fellow, if one wasn't too concerned about being the butt of a good joke. Nathaniel wondered briefly if he was the entertainment or if he should warn the unfortunate woman accompanying Eliot.

Eliot gestured to the woman. "Mr. Jenkins. May I introduce my sister-in-law, Miss Blakesley."

"Miss Blakesley." Nathaniel could not help but stare at poor Miss Blakesley. If ever the word spinster applied more he'd not met the woman. Here was a paragon of womanly failure. Her hair was pinned back in a widow's knot and she was dressed in hideous brown bombazine with buttons clear to her neck. She looked quite capable of taking a swatch to his backside for any impropriety.

She caught his eye and he couldn't help but feel that she was laughing at his perusal of her dress.

She said, "I prefer orange myself but it is so hard to find nowadays."

Nathaniel glanced to his right and saw no fewer than four orange dresses.

He said, "Oh, yes. Fashion."

A small smile lifted the corners of her mouth. Her eyes flicked down, taking in his conventional evening wear. Not out of date, but definitely not in fashion. Nathaniel preferred clothing that would be in style for more than a season, preferably a decade.

Miss Blakesley seemed to prefer clothing that would never be in style. One would save money, at least.

Rufus Eliot said, "Do you by any chance study the stars, Jenkins? It is Miss Blakesley's passion."

Knowing his duty, Nathaniel turned to her. "I am sorry to say I do not. What is it about the stars you enjoy, Miss Blakesley?"

"I can study them in peace and they always wear the same thing. Do you have a passion, Mr. Jenkins?"

"I have not had the luxury of late but I do enjoy fishing."

Rufus Eliot smiled. "A country

man."

Nathaniel nodded. "I prefer it. There are more fish there."

Miss Blakesley nodded. "And better smelling rivers."

"It does increase the pleasure somewhat."

She laughed. "Indeed. I find London terrible for star-gazing. It must be even less suited for fishing."

"I will admit that the thought of spending the day near the edge of the Thames leaves me quite cold." Nathaniel looked into her sparkling eyes and was interested despite himself. "Do you continue your star-gazing while in town, Miss Blakesley?"

She nodded. "It is a dismal business here but I keep up the habit. I have sketch after sketch of fog."

He smiled. "Do you find fog just as fascinating?"

"Not in the least. It is too transitory for my liking." She

cocked her head. "Somewhat like fashion, actually."

A laugh escaped him. Miss Blakesley smiled back at him, then flicked her eyes behind him and sighed. "It was nice to meet you, Mr. Jenkins. But my mother has spotted me and I fear neither one of us is safe. Once one reaches a certain age, one becomes a mother's pet project."

"I've noticed the phenomenon myself."

"Have you? Then I feel for you, Mr. Jenkins. If you'll excuse me."

"Certainly, Miss Blakesley. Eliot."

Nathaniel watched her walk quickly towards the other end of the room and thought he had never met a more curious woman.

Mary fluttered her fan. "Well?"

"I only spoke two sentences to him before Mama noticed and started making her way towards us."

"So? What did he say in those two sentences?"

"He likes the country and fishing. But does not care much for the stars."

"Who does, besides you? If that is what you are waiting for in a husband then you *will* die a spinster."

Olivia shook her head. "He does not need to share my passions. I simply wanted to take a measure of his character."

Rufus nodded towards the door. "He does not seem to like having his character measured. He's leaving."

Mary said, "Perhaps he is being a dutiful son and taking his mother home. That is Mrs. Jenkins he is escorting."

Olivia glanced quickly at the departing Mr. Jenkins. "Well, my two sentences with him did not gain me much information. There must be a better way of learning about a gentleman."

Mary smiled knowingly. "Perhaps Rufus can make some inquiries. Dear, can you find out if Mr. Jenkins would make a suitable brother-in-law?"

Olivia frowned. "Don't say anything so foolish in front of Mama. I will never hear the end of it." She looked at Rufus. "Could you? Discreetly."

He winked theatrically. "Leave it to me, Sis."

"I am doomed," Olivia said and began to lecture on the constellations as her mother swooped in with hope in her eyes.

Nathaniel helped his mother into the carriage wishing he could escape to his club. His mother would want to rehash the last hour, lady by lady. He wished, not for the first time, that he was not such a dutiful son.

She said, "Who was the woman you were talking to right before we left?"

"Miss Blakesley. Her brother-in-law and I belong to the same club."

"She's a little older, isn't she?"

"A bit, though I wouldn't say thirty. Should I warn her that you are getting desperate to marry me off to anyone not in braids?"

"I should think if she was nearing thirty I would need to warn you. I doubt the desperation I feel can compare to hers."

Nathaniel grunted, and for an instant felt sympathy for the poor woman. If her mother was anything like his, she must indeed be feeling desperate. He at least did not live under the same roof and could retire in peace, far away from her anxious schemings.

In truth though, Miss Blakesley had not seemed desperate. Interested, certainly. But also curious. She was not indelicate about her scrutiny but he felt it nonetheless. As an eligible bachelor, he had been appraised before. And as much as he did not appreciate the experience, he understood it. What woman would want to give her life and love to someone she did not know?

However, Miss Blakesley's scrutiny had been different. He, for once, had not felt like she was calculating his fortune but instead felt she was sincerely interested in knowing *him*. He had been slightly, and embarrassingly, aroused by her interest.

Though why he would be aroused by a woman wearing a dreary brown frock with a tight collar buttoned up to her neck, he did not know. She was definitely not your average young chit.

His mother smiled and gazed out the window. "She didn't seem quite as talkative as the other girls. You at least had conversation with her."

He nodded. "About fishing the Thames. And sketching the stars in London."

His mother blinked. "Well, that is

certainly a different kind of conversation then what you are used to." She paused. "She's not young, and certainly not frilly. Perhaps we've found a different species of fish, after all. Would you call her chatty?"

Nathaniel groaned and leaned his head back. His mother smiled, and wondered about Miss Blakesley.

Two

Miss Olivia Blakesley had made up her mind. After a few sleepless nights and a little sip from her father's brandy. Awful stuff.

Rufus had come back with an all clear on Mr. Jenkins. She wasn't going to give a stranger the keys to her family's downfall unless she was sure he wouldn't use them. One could never be sure but it appeared as if he wouldn't.

Mary, of course, had told everyone of her interest. They kept humming the wedding march under their breath whenever her mother was out of earshot.

Olivia had no interest in telling them her real plans for Mr. Nathaniel Jenkins.

She was going to seduce him. Or rather, have him seduce her. She wasn't at all sure how to go about it, her education so far teaching her how not to be seduced. And, she might add, she had been led to believe it would be a difficult task. Men apparently not being able to control their baser instincts.

But Olivia had never been accosted. Not once.

No suitor had ever tried to dally in a darkened corner, offer her a stroll in a deserted garden, or taken advantage of an accidental meeting.

She was starting to think the voracious appetites of the male species to be an exaggeration. Perhaps she should have chosen a rake after all.

If all else failed, she could always lower her standards.

She spotted Mr. Jenkins on the

dance floor, twirling another entirely too young woman in a decadent waltz. The Donner's Ball was quite the smash, despite a few disapproving looks for the choice of dance.

It was a bit crowded but Olivia hoped to take advantage of that. Sometime tonight she was going to corner Mr. Jenkins and proposition him.

She smoothed her skirt in a sudden nervous spurt of energy. If she was wrong about his character she would be a ruined old spinster by tomorrow morning.

On the bright side, it might be easier to catch a rake if she was ruined.

On the dark side, she might be the laughing-stock of the *ton*. Oh, wouldn't that be wonderful.

Well, nothing for it. All she had to lose was her reputation. Self-respect. Trust of her family.

Dear God, I'm a hoyden, she thought and went to position

herself for an accidental encounter.

Nathaniel didn't know what was worse, being twittered at by a brainless child or stared at without pause. He'd at least had experience with brainless chatter.

And she wasn't even flirting! Miss Blakesley simply stared. No coy smiles, silly fan work, fluttering lashes. Just watching him– sizing him up, he couldn't help but feel.

He wondered if she found him lacking. Was there something on his nose? His cravat in ruins? Surely his mother would have rushed over to save herself the embarrassment.

He excused himself from his partner, thankful that tonight there were men enough as dancing partners. He had done his duty; his mother could not fault him tonight. Although, unless he introduced her to a new bride this evening, she would anyway. Perhaps he would make his escape and leave his sister and brother-in-law to escort her home.

"Mr. Jenkins? Please excuse me for intruding on your thoughts."

He turned and found Miss Blakesley inches from him, staring.

"Miss Blakesley, forgive me. I did not see you in the crush."

She smiled slightly. "I do apologize. You looked quite ready to leave and there is a. . . a small matter I wish to discuss with you."

He nodded, looking down at her. Up close, she was prettier than he remembered– in a serious, studious way. From afar she looked ready to battle the world. But to his surprise he towered over her; her personality loomed much larger than her small frame. And her all-seeing eyes were a pale shade of blue.

"Shall we dance, Miss Blakesley?"

She looked at the dance floor longingly, then shook herself. "I would like that, Mr. Jenkins.

However, the matter I wish to discuss is a bit private."

Private? Was the girl trying to catch him? Being seen together in a compromising situation would certainly speed things along.

He said, "I'm afraid there is not much privacy offered tonight. A waltz may be the closest we can get."

"A waltz? Oh, yes. Well, perhaps that would work. Shall we?"

Nathaniel grinned down at her, offering his arm. "Why, thank you."

Miss Blakesley blushed, taking his arm. What was she up to? No gently bred lady had ever tracked him across a ball before, nor wished to speak to him in private.

Or stared at him with icy blue eyes, making him feel like an open book.

He led her once around the floor, noticing the rigid corset under her dress.

He said, "What was it you wished to speak about?"

Miss Blakesley cleared her throat and looked over his shoulder. "I want to assure you that I am in earnest. I can only imagine what you will think, but I. . . I would like you to seduce me."

Nathaniel missed a step and tripped over her foot. A blush rose again to her cheeks. "Perhaps waltzing wasn't a good idea."

He was silent while he tried to think of an appropriate response. Had she really just asked him to seduce her?

She glanced at him, her cheeks glowing, and he decided she *had.*

"Are you completely mad?"

She glanced at him quickly, then continued to stare over his shoulder. "No. I'm inexperienced and wish to change that. I had hoped you could help me."

"I hesitate to ask why out of all the men of your acquaintance you have chosen me to relieve you of your inexperience."

"You are not a rake."

"No?"

"No. Having been through eight seasons I assure you I can spot the type."

He couldn't stop his eyebrows from raising at her frank admission of eight seasons. He didn't know how old his mother was and his sister wouldn't admit to any age.

"Miss Blakesley, this is absurd. Even if I *were* a rake, I could not. . . assist you."

The waltz ended and Nathaniel escorted her off the floor.

She gripped his arm. "Teach me the acts of seduction, Mr. Jenkins."

He steered her to a blissfully empty corner and sat her in a chair rather abruptly.

"I don't think you know what you're asking," he said, taking another chair as far from her as possible and still be in the conversation.

"I assure you I do. But all my knowledge is second-hand. I would like to experience it myself."

Nathaniel muttered a curse word not intended for polite ears and crossed his legs. Good God, he was hard! Simply talking about the subject in a most clinical way he was tempted to haul Miss Blakesley out of her chair and ravish her senseless.

She wanted him to seduce her!

What was the world coming to.

"Miss Blakesley, this is highly irregular, and very definitely immoral. I must advise you to do as every other woman and find yourself a husband. You are a gently bred lady with a good reputation."

"And I am seven and twenty. Far too old to 'find myself a husband'."

"You are not so old; I would not have guessed a day past twenty-five."

One of her elegantly cynical eyebrows raised. "Fine. Would you marry me?"

Nathaniel pushed himself back in his chair. "Me? Miss Blakesley. . ."

"Exactly. I am too old and too set in my ways, with far too many freedoms–"

Nathaniel muttered, "Amen to that."

"–to make a good wife, and I doubt I would enjoy a husband. I would enjoy a lover though." She studied him a bit, eyeing his polished boots, the breeches molding his thighs, his hands clasped in his lap. "I would enjoy you."

Nathaniel cleared his throat.

"Miss Blakesley, I still can't help but think you don't know what you are asking, else you wouldn't be asking a practical stranger."

"It would be perfectly acceptable to marry you after such a short time. I don't see how this is any different."

What logic. If she couldn't tell the difference between marriage and what she was suggesting there was no hope he could point it out.

She said, "I'm willing to pay

you."

His mouth fell open. "Pardon?"

"I have access to the money saved for my dowry. I'm not willing to part with all of it, since you won't be marrying me, but I'll be able to pay what you think is fair."

Nathaniel felt his face go red. "You want to pay me? I am not a damn prostitute!"

Miss Blakesley blinked, then coughed discreetly. "I had not thought of it like that. Male prostitution? Would I call you a gentleman of the night?"

She chuckled and the low sound sent a chill down his spine.

He said, "You belong in Bedlam."

She chuckled again. "I did not mean you would be a prostitute. I would like you to seduce me, woo me, not just. . . you know."

"You want to pay me to woo you."

"Yes. This is my one chance; I think I should have it all. I would like to be courted. You can come calling, dance with me, escort me to the opera. My sisters were never so happy as when they were being pursued. I would like the same."

"And then presumably after I have wooed and won you, I would seduce you, and then jilt you in the eyes of the *ton* when I never see you again."

Miss Blakesley tipped her head. "I know it will cause a very minor stir but I will take the blame. I have no one to impress, while one day you will have to take a wife." She leaned forward, her expression thoughtful. "I would suggest girls a little older. Not too old, but not ones right out of the nursery. You seem to need a little heavier conversation than they can provide. Just a thought."

"Thank you for the advice, Miss Blakesley."

"You're welcome. Now where were we?"

"You were turning me into a rake."

"I wasn't!"

Nathaniel said, "That is what it sounds like to me. I court you, make you fall in love with me, take your innocence, and leave you. I can't think of a better definition than that. Perhaps you should find a man with more experience with that than I."

She stared at him, her forehead wrinkled in consternation. "But I specifically do not want a rake. I do have my reputation to consider and I don't want even a breath of scandal surrounding my family. Surely no one would think that you had compromised me."

"I hesitate to ask what you mean by that."

"Well. . . I mean. . . You seem quite. . . Oh, dear. I didn't mean to attack your virility."

Nathaniel guffawed. "I didn't know you were attacking my virility."

"I just meant you have a reputation yourself. You never let

your passions overwhelm you. You don't drink or gamble to excess and you are quite discreet with your. . . lovers."

He stared at her. Where this woman got her ideas and information from he didn't know, but she had to be the most informed woman in the *ton*.

Miss Blakesley smiled a little at him. "I do have five brothers-in-law, Mr. Jenkins. I usually can wheedle what I need out of them."

"And I assume you have their blessings for this insane scheme of yours?"

"They all agree you are excellent husband material so I will have to assume you are excellent seducer material as well."

Nathaniel rubbed his forehead, thinking her circular arguments would land him in Bedlam as well.

"Miss Blakesley, I must admit that though I am intrigued by your proposition, I must decline. My honor would not allow me to compromise you in such a fashion."

Her shoulders seemed to sag a little but she rallied quickly. "Of course. I do understand, Mr. Jenkins. Your refusal tells me I was right about your character." She smiled wryly. "I shall have to find someone with not so many morals. Could you recommend any other gentleman of your acquaintance?"

He stood sharply. "Certainly not. This entire affair is a foolish idea. Find yourself a husband."

Miss Blakesley stood as well. "As I have told you, that is impossible. I have a few extremely bad habits and I do not desire a husband."

He took a step closer, ignoring her sad eyes and pert nose. "I'm afraid, Miss Blakesley, that you must be ruined without my help."

She glanced at his lips and whispered, "That's a shame, Mr. Jenkins."

He stared at the maddening woman, then turned briskly away. The faster he got away from her the better.

Honor was beginning to seem a poor consolation prize for what she was offering.

Three

A week later, Nathaniel waited impatiently as his carriage slowly wound its way to the Hamilton's. He had prepared for this ball with more excitement than he had felt in a long time. Possibly ever, as he wasn't more than a passable dancer and the conversations had always run toward fashion. Now, however, there was Miss Blakesley. What scandalous dialogue she would insist on spouting while buttoned up to the neck, he had no idea. But he did not doubt it would be amusing. And intriguing. And arousing.

He had thought of little else than her this last week, playing again their conversation. No wonder. He had never before been approached by a woman to ruin her. He could in all honesty say she did not look mad. Or devious. Or even passionate. And yet, she was all three.

She looked like the scholarly spinster that she was. But underneath she was so much more. He was looking forward to her shocking him again tonight.

Oh, he had no intention of taking her up on her offer; he would talk her out of her madness if she continued to insist upon it. But he could not seem to stop thinking about it or her.

His mother intruded on his thoughts. "You look quite eager tonight, Nathaniel."

He immediately dropped the curtain and sat back on the seat. "Perhaps I have accepted the necessity of all these social engagements."

"Mmm. What's her name?"

Nathaniel grinned at his mother, who sat back with an expression of shock on her face. He laughed. "Come, Mother. I can't be such an ogre that a grin throws you."

She composed herself. "Of course not. But you must admit this is quite a change from last week when I practically had to drag you."

He nodded. "On reflection, I have decided I enjoyed myself immensely last week. And I have every intention of doing so again." He skewered her with a stare. "But I do not want you jumping to conclusions about every young lady I come in contact with."

His mother opened her fan, waving it idly. "You could do worse than find someone who excites you, Nathaniel."

It was true. However, he doubted his mother would approve of the lady if she knew why he was excited.

As if reading his mind she said, "If it is Miss Blakesley, I think it a good match. She does seem to have a certain indescribable character about her."

"Yes, she is fascinating."

"And really dear, don't think too much on the age. It is true she is not fresh from the schoolroom but she is still young enough. She is from a good, quiet, respectable family."

Nathaniel snorted. If Miss Blakesley was anything it was not good, quiet, or respectable.

Olivia searched the crowded ballroom with little enjoyment. Since Mr. Jenkins had so very effectively dismissed her, she had been hard pressed to get excited about the project.

It didn't help to know that he was

right– it was a foolish idea. And the chances of her succeeding were shrinking every day. She needed to find a good, decent man and ask him to act in a reprehensible way.

Foolishness, indeed.

She hadn't actually thought he would reject her. What man could ignore his baser passions when offered an unplucked flower on a platter?

Obviously, when it was her unplucked flower, it was easy.

At this rate she was going to have to find a rake after all. And one who didn't have high expectations.

It was turning into a thoroughly depressing affair.

Olivia stiffened the instant Mr. Jenkins walked in the door. She didn't even have to see him to know he was there. She pasted a smile on her face and turned to say something witty to her sister, hoping he would ignore her for the night.

Mary poked her in the ribs. "Ooh,

look who's just arrived. He's looking over here."

"He is not."

"He is. And his mother is staring at you."

Olivia's face flushed and she whipped her head around to find both of them watching her. Mr. Jenkins nodded, looking almost happy to be there. Wasn't that just wonderful for him.

His mother looked quite intrigued. Even worse.

Olivia couldn't imagine he had told his mother anything, but he wasn't exactly being subtle.

Mary whispered behind her fan. "He looks almost enamored, Livvy. What did you speak of last week?"

Olivia refused to blush again. "Nothing, really. I didn't talk of fashion though. Perhaps he's simply never met a woman who didn't know a flounce from a ruffle before."

Mary snorted. "I'm sure he hasn't and I'm sure that's not why he's coming over here right now."

Olivia took a quick breath, ignoring her speeding heart. Hopefully he wasn't coming to give her another set-down.

"Mrs. Eliot. Miss Blakesley. Would you still have a waltz free?"

Olivia ignored Mary's wide smile. If she could have, she would have ignored Nathaniel Jenkins and his unexpected dance offer as well. "Yes, thank you."

He bowed slightly and left. Mary's fan went into convulsions and she sing-songed, "Olivia has a suitor."

By the time Mr. Jenkins came for her, she was ready. She would not blush again. She had propositioned him for goodness sake; she could certainly dance with him without turning red as a cherry.

The music started, the couples began dancing, and he said, "I hope you have given up on your extremely foolish idea, Miss Blakesley."

So much for gently breaking into the subject. She eyed him coolly. "Of course not. A child learning to walk does not quit after the first tumble."

"You must agree this is a little more foolhardy, and certainly more sinister, than learning to walk."

"The principles are the same no matter the endeavor, Mr. Jenkins."

His eyes flashed and he brought her closer for a spin. "Very well. Then tell me who you are considering."

Olivia sniffed. "Why?"

"Because I am an excellent judge of character. And who else will you be able to ask?"

Olivia considered. It would be nice to have a second opinion. And he would have heard more about the darker side of a gentleman's character than she. She hadn't the heart to go ask her brothers-in-law anymore, they teased her endlessly about Mr. Jenkins.

"Fine. Mr. James Woolthy."

"Jimmy? Too fat. He'll have no stamina for the activities you have planned."

Olivia bit her tongue and glared at him. He seemed entirely too cheerful.

"Mr. Marcus Matthews. He is not fat at all."

"No, but he is too young. He'll not have enough experience to make the experiment worthwhile."

"Mr. Simon Rawling."

"Too much in love with the bottle. He won't be able to get the old boy up."

Olivia pondered that for a moment. Mr. Jenkins watched her, his fingers gripping tighter around her waist.

She said, "Well, I fear my options are becoming quite limited. It seems I am left with Mr. Damien St. Martins, the youngest son of Lord Waverley."

Mr. Jenkins tripped over his own foot. "Miss Blakesley! He is a rake of the worst kind. Your reputation won't survive that scandal."

"Can you think of anyone better?"

He stared over her shoulder and sighed. "I suppose it shall have to be me."

Olivia huffed. "If it will be too much of a bother, don't put yourself out, sir."

He glanced at her. "Was I not enthusiastic enough for you, Miss Blakesley?"

"No, you weren't. And if I do decide to go ahead with you, I would like an assurance that you'll do better in the future."

Mr. Jenkins choked back a laugh. "Of course, Miss Blakesley. It was thoughtless of me. How can I show you my enthusiasm? Shall we take a stroll through the gardens?"

"Are you funning me, Mr. Jenkins?"

"Of course not, Miss Blakesley. I'm simply wondering if you would like to sample the goods before you decide."

He'd meant it as a joke, surely, but Olivia thought it a sensible idea. What if they were incompatible?

She said, "Perhaps a quick nip outside for some fresh air would be beneficial, thank you."

Mr. Jenkins stared at her, then shook himself. "Remind me not to offer any more inappropriate suggestions. You seem to run away with them."

Olivia merely looked at him. He was either going to seduce her or he wasn't, and even if there were no other suitors in line for her she would not be desperate. She could have married long ago if she'd been willing to settle for just anybody.

The waltz slowed and ended, and Olivia continued to look at him.

He cleared his throat. "Very well. Shall we take a stroll, Miss Blakesley?"

"Thank you, it is a bit warm in here."

Mr. Jenkins escorted her to the

terrace where, unfortunately, two matrons sat taking the air and watching another couple. He led her to the other side, well away from prying ears if not prying eyes.

He said, "I dare not take you into the gardens with those two watching."

Olivia quietly sighed. "I understand, Mr. Jenkins. And I appreciate your care for my reputation."

He grasped her hand lightly between his, rubbing it gently. "I would like to take you into those gardens and kiss you senseless, though. I wouldn't want you thinking I was unenthusiastic."

She gaped at him. "You *want* to kiss me?"

A light twinkled in his eyes. "I would not have agreed to this crazy scheme if I didn't." He lightly touched her, right below her ear. "I want to nuzzle you here, surround myself in your scent."

Olivia cleared her throat. "That

does sound inter–"

"And slowly unbutton this god-awful dress until I can see the tops of your pert breasts peeking through. I think they would fit in my hands perfectly."

Her nipples beaded as he gazed at them and Olivia glanced behind him to make sure no one had heard.

His finger slid inside the cuff of her sleeve and stroked her soft skin.

"In fact, I think I'd get rid of this dress entirely. I'd start here at your wrist and kiss and nibble my way up your arm, stopping to lick the crook of your elbow, and leisurely pull you closer until your breasts crushed against my chest. And then I'd kiss your lips, softly at first, gently, feeling the softness press warmly back. And you'd open your mouth to sigh and I'd slip my tongue in to play with yours."

Olivia jumped, staring at his mouth, and whispered, "Is that pleasant?"

One side of his mouth quirked. "Oh, yes."

It didn't sound like it would be but Olivia trusted that he knew what he was about. One hoped he had more experience than she. He couldn't possibly have less.

"What is also pleasant is if you circle your arms around my neck and kiss me back, your body stretching along mine, my hands cupping your derriere and pulling you tightly against my erection."

"Mr. Jenkins!" She looked behind him again, hoping no one had heard *that.* Satisfied that they were still safe she glanced down between them, hoping for a glimpse. "Do you have one now, sir?"

He smiled dangerously. "Would you like to find out?"

When she gave a jerky nod, he guided her hand to his breeches. Olivia's heart beat furiously and the need for air seemed to have deserted her. She looked up into his face, saw passion and want, and understood power for the first time in her life. She had done that to him.

She trailed her hand lower, searching for she knew not what. Her hand brushed his hard member and his muscles shook.

She jerked her hand back. "Did I hurt you?"

He shook his head. "No. But perhaps this wasn't a good idea after all. I don't want to have to ravish you with an audience."

Satisfaction stole through Olivia. "Do you want to ravish me?"

"Miss Blakesley, you are two steps away from being swept into the garden and seduced quite thoroughly."

The light laughter of another couple coming out to enjoy the air intruded upon them and Mr. Jenkins stepped back. His heat left her and Olivia realized just how hot he had been.

He adjusted the front of his breeches discreetly and cleared his throat. "I had meant to shock you out of this mad idea, Miss Blakesley, not incite myself."

Olivia shook herself. "If that was indeed your plan, Mr. Jenkins, you failed magnificently. But if we are to continue, I think there will have to be a few rules."

He paused for a moment as if he was willing his better sense to take over. She held her breath.

He nodded and she began to breathe again.

He said, "Yes, and number one will be to use our Christian names."

That seemed quite scandalous. Even her mother still called her father Mr. Blakesley. Of course, the whole affair was quite scandalous.

"Agreed, but only in private."

"Agreed. Olivia."

Olivia's stomach flopped and she looked up into his brightly burning eyes. She had thought him quite ordinary looking, that was one of the reasons she had chosen him, but at that moment she would be hard pressed to find someone more arresting. He seemed quite powerful, manly.

Dear Lord, she would have to go back inside to cool down the way they were going.

"Rule number two," he growled. "There will not be any other men around while I am pursuing you."

Olivia fanned herself. "Of course not. A true experiment would require a comparison, but this is an experience. I will be delighted to simply have the opportunity."

And she would not forget that it had been hard enough to find one suitable and willing seducer. She would not bet with herself that she could find two.

The next dance started up and Olivia reluctantly let him lead her inside. "I have not told you any of my rules, Mr. . . Nathaniel."

He escorted her to her sister, sketched a bow, and grinned at her. "I am sure there will be ample time for you to read me the list tomorrow morning, Miss Blakesley. Until then."

She watched him walk the length of the ballroom, thinking she had picked the best of the lot. At least if one was comparing backsides. And seductive capabilities!

"Olivia?" Mary poked her with the fan.

"Hmm?"

"I said, a waltz and the terrace? My, oh my. He is coming calling tomorrow?"

"It would seem so." Olivia grinned at her sister. "I may be in need of more fresh air."

Mary laughed. "Of course, sister dear. You do look a bit peaked."

Olivia rushed to an open window, reminding herself not to break into song and dance. She was a respectable young lady. She could not create such a spectacle of herself.

She settled for vigorously waving her fan, hoping it hid her too-large smile and too-warm cheeks.

She, Miss Olivia Blakesley, spinster extraordinaire, had found herself a seducer.

Four

"Rule number one: You can tell no one of our arrangement."

Nathaniel escorted Olivia through the park on his arm, her maid following discreetly. Since this was the first time her maid had ever acted as chaperone, she was doing remarkably well at keeping nearly out of sight. Olivia wondered idly if her mother had told the maid to stay as far away as possible. Olivia wouldn't put it past her mother to think a slight scandal might move a marriage along.

"Of course, Olivia. A gentleman does not kiss and tell."

62

She nodded. Yet one had to wonder how all the gossip started if not for a little kiss and tell. She knew of at least two young ladies whose reputations had been ruined by hearsay.

She would have to trust Nathaniel that he would not ruin her. Or, at least not tell anyone that he had ruined her.

"Rule number two: I may at any time decide not to go through with our agreement and you will respect that. I will, of course, still pay you."

Nathaniel stopped in his tracks. "Do you think you'll change your mind?"

"Well, I don't know, do I? What if I find the marital act terrifying? One hears so many stories. I just would like your assurance that you'll stop if I ask."

"You won't find it terrifying, Olivia. Thrilling, certainly. And you won't want me to stop." He pulled her hand back through his arm and continued walking. "However, if you wish to stop, I will. But mean it if you say it. Starting and stopping is very hard on a man."

"I will certainly take that into consideration, Nathaniel. Hopefully it will not be necessary."

Nathaniel nodded. "And you won't be paying me."

"I certainly will."

"No, you won't. I will not be a paid courtesan, a prostitute, or your mistress. . . master. . . Anyhow, I will not be paid."

"Then why are you doing this? There's nothing in it for you. I will not be charity." Olivia glared at him. "Don't laugh at me."

"I'm not laughing at you. Women are paid for this kind of service because it is not always pleasurable for them. For a man it is. That will be my payment."

"Hmm. I still think you should be paid."

"No. That is final."

Olivia sniffed, watching the other

couples walking along the green. They all looked quite young. And hopeful. And young.

And most definitely innocent. She doubted any of them were having a conversation quite like theirs.

"There is one thing you haven't thought of, Olivia. What if you become pregnant?"

She continued to look away from Nathaniel as she answered. She was really getting quite tired of blushing in front of him. "I have thought of it. I read somewhere that there is a precaution a man can take to prevent pregnancy. Do you know of it?"

Nathaniel cleared his throat. "Yes. It isn't foolproof, though."

Olivia had been afraid it wasn't. Was it worth the risk? She took a deep breath. It was. If worse came to worst, she could visit relatives until the baby was due. She had five sisters, one of them would surely raise her baby if need be. Mary would, definitely.

"I hesitate to ask how you know such things, Olivia."

"I do have–"

"And don't tell me you have five brothers-in-law. I doubt any of them would have mentioned such a thing."

She glanced at him, noting his dark expression. "Almost anything can be found in a book, Nathaniel."

"Not any books you should be reading."

True. She had an extremely naughty book hidden under a floorboard in her room. She might let him look at it when they knew each other a little better. She had a few questions for him.

"Well, I've read quite a few things I shouldn't have. I will accept full responsibility should something unfortunate happen."

He muttered, "Bloody hell," and she ignored it. She was putting him in an extremely stressful situation after all.

She said, "Would you like me to

pay you after all? I understand the method is not so pleasurable for the man."

He was turning a bit red and his collar seemed to be bothering him. "No, you will not pay me."

She patted his arm. "Of course, Nathaniel. I did not mean to insult your manly pride."

This was really turning into more work than Olivia had planned.

They resumed walking and he said, "Was that the list, then? You only have two rules?"

"I did have a third one, but after last night's demonstration I am no longer worried about your devotion to the project. I think we'll do quite well together. Although, I'm certain I'll think of more rules as situations arise."

"I'm certain you will."

"I would like to know why you changed your mind, though. You seemed quite put out with me when I originally asked."

"You surprised me, Olivia. It was

like having a dog come up and ask for its dinner. Wholly unsuspected."

Olivia turned to stare at him. "Are you comparing me to a dog, sir? A talking dog? Surely it could not have been as unbelievable as that."

Nathaniel grimaced. "That wasn't what I meant. Of course I was not comparing you to a dog."

"It sounded like you were."

"I was not expecting a gently bred lady to proposition me. I was expecting you to talk about your stars, or since you wanted to be private, I was expecting you to try and compromise yourself."

Olivia nodded. "I see. You expected a bark and instead found I could speak. Do the ladies often try and compromise themselves with you?"

"Not often, no."

"You seem to have a low regard for my sex, Mr. Jenkins."

"Or a very high regard for dogs."

"I wonder, sir, why you are not

married. It has left me quite baffled."

He bent his head and laughed. His shoulders shook as he quietly gave in to the inevitable. Olivia tried very hard to keep her lips pursed.

"I apologize, Olivia. My charm has deserted me, it seems. If my mother knew I had just compared a lady to a dog, I'm sure she would disown me completely."

"Which I'm sure you would deserve."

"I would indeed. How may I make this up to you?"

Olivia patted his arm. "Let us simply forgive and forget. I believe the situation we find ourselves in will lend itself to the occasional social blunder."

"Thank you, my dear. But perhaps a rest in this gazebo will show I am not completely without manners."

"Thank you, Nathaniel. It is getting a bit warm. I've always thought gazebos so nice to cool down in."

Nathaniel grinned, pulling her into his arms as soon as they entered. "I don't think you'll do much cooling down in this one."

Her surprised look congratulated him as he slowly bent his head and touched his lips to hers. He gently flicked her upper lip with his tongue, expertly guiding it in at her gasp. His tongue flicked hers playfully.

Olivia grasped his lapels, breathing faster, daringly touching her tongue to his.

"Oh, Nathaniel. That *is* pleasant."

He traced the back of her corset, sliding his fingers under her arms, tempting himself. She murmured something and stepped closer, crushing her chest against his. Nathaniel traced the rise of her breast and groaned.

Olivia's maid called out and he pushed her away quickly. Her chest heaved as she tried to gulp down air.

She said, "So, this is the fascination with gazebos."

"Yes, but we may be seen at any moment by someone other than your maid."

"I think that is part of the fascination."

He smiled as they exited and found her maid waiting, pointedly looking at the trees.

Nathaniel said, "Well, my dear. I believe you requested an escort to the opera. Will you join me?"

She wrinkled her nose, then squared her shoulders. "I did want the full experience and a night at the opera does seem *de rigueur* for courting couples. Thank you, Nathaniel, that will be. . . wonderful."

Nathaniel had lost his mind. Or rather, he kept losing it whenever he went near Olivia Blakesley. He had meant to talk her out of getting seduced, not talk himself into it. But here he was, courting her, wooing her.

Taking her to the opera!

The last time he'd let his pants do the talking for him, he'd been eighteen and had come home with a black eye. If he continued with this mad scheme, he'd be coming home with a bullet in his gut from one of her brothers-in-law.

Madness. She was a gently-bred woman. An oddly-reared, stubborn, passionate, intelligent woman.

And he couldn't help but feel that if he refused her, she would find some other man. Another man who might hurt her or her family.

He shook his head in disgust. He was grasping for straws here, any excuse that would let him do what he wanted.

Because he wanted her. Wanted her more than he'd wanted a woman in a very long time.

He had not felt so excited to be alive since his father had died. She shocked him, amused him, aroused him.

He wouldn't hurt her, as some other men might. He would give her what she wanted; an experience to last a lifetime. No one would know, no one would be hurt. He could go ahead with his conscience clear.

And he would gag the voice in his head that was telling him that this would be the final nail in her spinster's coffin.

Mary arrived later that evening to join them for dinner and stole up to Olivia's bedroom to hear all the juicy details one couldn't tell one's mother. Since there were far too many juicy details one couldn't tell one's sister as well, Olivia glossed over her morning outing and went straight to the next planned encounter.

"You want to go to the opera?" Mary looked at her oddly. "Since when?"

"Since a handsome man asked me to attend with him."

"Ah, of course. I should have expected that. Well, I'll certainly join you, and Rufus, too. He loves the music." Mary looked at Olivia's pained face and laughed. "You did know there was singing involved, didn't you?"

"I suspected. Is it awful?"

"It's nothing like Prudence and her screeching, if that's what you're asking. You should ask Rufus to explain it before you go. I've actually started to enjoy it."

"Poor Rufus, to be married into our unmusical family."

"Mmm. Perhaps I should warn your Mr. Jenkins."

"Perhaps I should bop you over the head with my telescope."

Mary tsked at her. "So violent. Never fear, I won't say a word to him about that. What will you be wearing? Mama says she almost got you to the dressmakers this week, but lost you to a bookseller on the way."

"I told her before we went that I didn't need any new dresses."

Mary looked down at Olivia's grey bombazine and raised an eyebrow. "Grey is not your color, Livvy. It makes you look deathly. I think you should take Mama up on the offer and get a nice spring yellow. You'd look lovely."

Olivia made a face and gagged. "Yellow? Be serious, Mary. I am nearly eight and twenty. No spinster should wear bright yellow. It would just be sad."

Mary looked at her crossly. "You are not a spinster, Olivia Blakesley. I hate when you say so."

Olivia sighed. "I am. And what's more I don't mind. I don't mind grey bombazine, either. I need never worry that I'll stain it."

"That's because it's ugly and no one would care if you burnt it. And I doubt Mr. Jenkins thinks you a spinster."

"Mr. Jenkins is not exactly in the first flush of youth either."

Mary laughed. "I don't think you can say that about men, Livvy. He is more mature."

Olivia agreed. He certainly was. And she got the distinct impression he liked her ugly dresses. He certainly talked encouragingly enough about getting her out of them.

She smiled as she followed Mary down to dinner. Even despite the looming threat of the opera, she could not wait until she could see Nathaniel again. He had already exceeded her greatest expectations.

She would just have to remember not to mention any more activities that she did not want to participate in. He was entirely too good a listener.

Five

The opera house was filled to the rafters with perfumed ladies and foppish men. Even with her blind fashion eye, Olivia could tell that here was where the *ton* fawned themselves. Striped pantaloons, cherry red lips, and powdered wigs. The women were even worse. One woman's hat looked as if it was about to fly away.

Mary looked at her face and laughed. "Regretting the bombazine now?"

"No. I was thinking it an improvement over most of the costumes here."

Nathaniel bent to whisper in Olivia's ear. "Have you never been to the opera, Olivia? I should have warned you."

"And I should have expected something like this. I knew there was a reason I'd never come before."

"Well, I hope the music is to your liking."

She kept a purposefully hopeful expression on her face. "They can't come just for the fashion, can they? I expect to be dazzled by beautiful singing and an emotional story."

Nathaniel laughed. "Is that a quote from the Times? If not, I believe your interests lie in the wrong field. You should become a critic. Do you speak German, then?"

Olivia frowned at him. "German?"

"This opera is in German."

"What, the singing? All of it?" She turned to Rufus. "You forgot to mention that."

He folded his pamphlet, laughing at her. "I thought you would guess by the title."

"I thought that was a gimmick. You told me it was beautiful and emotional; how was I to guess it was in German?"

Nathaniel pulled her away gently. "Come, my dear. Let's find our seats, shall we?"

"Do you come much, Nathaniel?"

"I confess, no."

Olivia followed him, secretly pleased that he did not regularly attend. And even more pleased that he had gone to the effort to take her. She smiled pleasantly at him. She would try to enjoy this experience knowing she wasn't likely to be subjected to it again.

Despite her sister's assurance, she could not imagine a beautiful melody, only torturous screeching. Thankfully, her mother had wisely chosen other accomplishments for her daughters to exhibit. One's ears were blissfully left alone by painting.

The four of them sat and Olivia leaned toward Mary and whispered, "How long is this supposed to last?"

Mary spoke behind her fan. "Three hours."

Olivia stared at her incredulously. "Of singing? Nothing but singing? In German?"

"There's an intermission where you can walk around and look at everyone's pretty dresses."

Olivia glared at her. No wonder she had never come to the opera before. Music and fashion, her two most favorite subjects.

Less than half an hour after the curtain rose, she glanced at Rufus. He sat forward in his chair, listening in rapture to the music. She wished she could hear what he so obviously enjoyed, but she hadn't a musical bone in her body. The only one of her sisters who could sing at all decently was Eugenia, and that was only through hours and hours of tortuous practice.

Give her the beautifully silent stars any day.

Olivia peeked at Nathaniel, half afraid he was in bliss himself. Though why she should care was beyond her. He wasn't really courting her. She wouldn't have to spend years accompanying him to the opera if he did enjoy it so.

Nonetheless, she let out a sigh of relief at his carefully neutral face.

He glanced at her and Olivia couldn't help but feel that they shared a moment of complete understanding and togetherness. She felt a twinge of regret that it could not last, but then shook herself. She would not poison this experience. Even if this had been a true courtship, it would end anyhow. She had enough married sisters to know that the thrill would fade. She would simply enjoy it while it lasted.

She was startled when

Nathaniel's hand found hers in the darkness. His thumb began to draw lazy patterns on her glove and she suppressed a shiver. She glanced at him but found he was suddenly quite fascinated with the show.

All of a sudden she was finding it quite exciting as well.

The beating of her heart drowned out all other sound as he continued to fondle her suddenly sensitive fingers. Her breath came faster and her stomach flipped and flopped. She fanned herself vigorously; the room had become inexplicably warm. She noticed a slight smirk on Nathaniel's face; the man needed a taste of his own medicine.

She began to fondle *his* fingers–stroking the long lengths, encircling the thickness. His breath hitched and she feared there was a little smirk on her face now. She glanced at him and met his eyes. They were bright and shining and he smiled a little at her. His own fingers once again sought to take control of the situation and she choked back her laugh as they fought for fondling dominance.

The longer she and Nathaniel courted the more she thought how well suited they were together. He was quite the most wonderful gentleman she'd ever gotten to know. They had the same interests, the same non-interests, and he made even the most head-pounding evening fly by. Every once in a while she thought it was a shame this was not a real courtship. Would they suit for real?

Of course, it wouldn't be very fair to him if she started thinking and acting like this was a real courtship. They had a deal and marriage wasn't part of it. She had propositioned him, so it wasn't likely he still thought her a proper young lady fit for a gentleman.

Intermission came quickly enough. Nathaniel's hand fiddling had kept her quite occupied, but she still begged Mary to leave early when they visited the lady's withdrawing room. Hand fiddling, while quite exhilarating, could not silence the interminable screeching.

"No. You asked us to accompany you, and Rufus has been so excited to come. We can't leave halfway through."

"I don't understand how he can be so passionate about it."

"None of us can understand what you find so all-consuming about the stars, yet we let you get on with it."

Olivia could think of quite a few instances where her family had not left her alone in peace to study her stars. Yet, she knew that Rufus felt quite passionate about music and she wouldn't want to deny him the pleasure. No matter how much it made her want to yell.

Mary said, "Besides, aren't you enjoying sitting so close to your Mr. Jenkins?"

"I am. But he doesn't seem to be enjoying himself so much either."

"At least you have that in

common. You won't have to attend with him in the future if neither of you enjoys it. Rufus says Mr. Jenkins prefers the country; you two can squirrel away to the countryside and be happy forevermore."

"The stars are clearer in the country. Town is all about fashion and gossip. I dare say this will be my last season here."

Mary grinned at her, happy. "I dare say it will be, too."

Olivia shook her head. "Even if nothing comes of Mr. Jenkins. I am about ready for spinster-hood."

Mary glared at her. "I will be ever so grateful when I no longer have to hear you call yourself a spinster. I am quite tired of it."

They left the lady's room and found themselves in quite a crush. They wound their way through to the gentlemen and Olivia could hear whispers and laughter. It was mostly gossip about fashion, but then she heard ". . .grey bombazine. . ." and realized it was she they were laughing about.

She smiled at such foolishness. She really did not understand what the fuss was about. She had dressed appropriately for the opera, if not fashionably.

". . .Jenkins doing with her?"

". . .do much better. . ."

". . .joke? Not like him. . ."

And she stopped smiling. Would his reputation suffer because of his supposed interest in her? At least no one could believe that Nathaniel was really courting her. Why would they? He was a solid gentleman with a solid fortune, he could have any woman he wished. He wouldn't choose to court a set-in-her-ways old maid. Oh, if they only knew the real reason he was here with her.

It was good he was such an honorable man. He would never tell anyone of their arrangement, that much she was sure of. When their arrangement came to an end, no one would think anything but that he had come to his senses and stopped pursuing such an unsuitable match.

She had benefited extraordinarily from his attention. She had experienced walking the green, flirtatious dancing, attending the opera, and been the object of a man's studied attention. It was getting hard for her to pretend it wasn't for real, and it seemed it was getting hard for others to ignore his attention as well. She hadn't meant to make anyone believe they had an attachment, least of all herself. She had simply wanted to know what it felt like to be wanted. Now she knew.

She also knew it was time to end the public courtship. She did not want his reputation to suffer from their association. She liked him far too well to cause him any harm.

At last the opera ended and they escaped. Nathaniel kept her close, ostensibly to guide her through the masses of people.

He said, "That was an experience I won't be quick to forget."

"Nor I. Thank you for suffering through it for me."

"Of course, Olivia. I did enjoy parts of it, though I hope we won't have to again for quite some time."

She shook her head. "Once was more than enough for me. But thank you, Nathaniel. This has been a wonderful courtship."

"Do you consider yourself wooed and won, then?"

She laughed, squeezing his arm. "I do, indeed." She paused, looking away. "But I wonder when the next part will come."

"I admit I've been hesitating."

"Why?"

"I've been hoping you would change your mind."

She scowled at him. "I won't."

"And also because once a couple unites, it changes their relationship. Sweet kisses and passionate embraces are no longer enough, the act itself becomes all important. It is very hard to go back to what one was before. . . Are you sure you want to continue, Olivia?"

As they stepped outside, the cool air made her shiver. She took a deep breath.

"Yes. That was what we agreed to, Nathaniel. I want to know. I want to know why the act becomes so important. I want to know why passion grips men's souls and makes women go all aflutter." She looked up at him and whispered. "Please show me."

He stared in silence at the line of carriages, then chuckled. "Will you be watching the stars tonight?"

Olivia glanced at the foggy sky, then smiled at him. "I expect not for long."

Nathaniel smiled, too. "No, not for long."

Six

If Mr. Nathaniel Jenkins didn't get here soon, Olivia was going to beat him with her telescope. They would find him bludgeoned to death and her only excuse would be that he'd promised to seduce her and hadn't. Could anyone blame her? Disown her certainly, but not blame her.

She had rushed outside as soon as it was dark– eager and expectant. That had been a good three hours ago and she was tired. The thrill had worn down to a dull aching in her stomach.

Perhaps he had changed his

mind. He was a gentleman after all. He had been taught from birth to never dally with another gentleman's daughter. One only married those.

She should have paid him. Then he would've had to come back to seduce her. She should have made him swear on his honor.

"The way you're glaring at that chimney makes me think I'm late."

Olivia jumped out of her chair, half out of fright, half out of righteous indignation.

"Yes, you're late. I've been out here for three hours. I'm freezing, my lower extremities have fallen asleep, and you've made me wait so long that I am not interested in you or anything you think you can teach me." She took a breath, pacing in front of him.

Nathaniel watched her with the intensity of a lion-tamer, his eyes following her ragged pacing.

"I apologize, Olivia. I should have been more specific. I didn't want to come when anyone would be awake."

Olivia hastily lowered her voice to a whisper. "Well, everyone has been asleep for a good while. I think I'll join them."

Nathaniel caught her wrist as she swept by him. "Olivia, wait."

She stopped, refusing to look at him, and wished the ache in her stomach would go away. She had not felt this ill since her coming-out.

Nathaniel slowly pulled her to the chair, settled himself, arranged her on his lap, and draped the blanket around them. He held her, his chin resting on her head, and said nothing.

Olivia relaxed unwillingly against him, his heat warming her. She breathed deeply and the scent of horse and man and bay filled her. Men smelled so differently than women. They smelled warmer somehow. Or perhaps they just felt warmer. She'd been held by her mother before, and she'd hugged her sisters. None of them had been so hot. Nathaniel's heat almost burned her.

She was getting a bit warm under the blanket.

Nathaniel's armed snaked around her waist, holding her closer.

"You can change your mind."

"I don't want to change my mind, I just wish I hadn't had so much time to think about it."

Olivia turned to face him, watching him in the moonlight. "May I kiss you?"

He smiled slightly and his armed tightened around her. "Yes."

Her heart pounded and her breath came faster. He had always kissed her before. It was all well and good to be seduced, but sometimes a woman had to take control. Otherwise, there was too much time for thinking.

She leaned forward and brushed his lips. Again and again she ran her closed lips gently against his.

They were soft, gliding smoothly against her own. She moved to his cheek, brushing her lips back and forth.

"You shaved."

She felt him smile, but he remained silent.

She stood, warmed by his heat, warmed by her own. She leaned over him, running her lips over his nose, slipping across his lashes and his closed eyes. His hands grasped lightly around her waist, caressing down her hips and thighs, and up around her rib-cage, gently nudging her breasts. Her breath caught.

He rose swiftly, wrapping the blanket around her. "Stay here a moment."

He knelt by his saddle-bags, pulling out a thick blanket and spreading it on the small deck. He placed a thinner blanket on top, then held his hand out to her, motioning for her to come. In his hand was a small red rose.

She walked toward him slowly, taking the rose and inhaling the sweet scent. She whispered, "Thank you, Nathaniel. This is more than I expected."

"You wanted to be wooed and seduced, Olivia. I am a man of my word."

She smiled, ignoring the butterflies in her stomach. She knelt on the blanket beside him and he took her hand, pulling her to press against him knee to chest.

He kissed her cheek and lips and whispered, "You wanted to learn the art of seduction, Miss Blakesley?"

"I believe I called it the acts of seduction."

He nibbled her bottom lip. "You'll learn that, too."

He leaned back, pulling her along until he was lying down with her on top. His hands cupped her bottom and she jumped a little, then laughed self-consciously. One of her knees lodged between his and she felt his rising passion pressing hard against her thigh.

Olivia pushed up a little. "May I touch it?"

Nathaniel chuckled. "I am your humble servant, Miss Blakesley. You may do whatever you wish with me."

She ran her hands down his torso, coming to stroke his erection. He inhaled sharply.

She jerked her hand back. "Did I hurt you?"

He shook his head, grabbing her hands and pressing them firmly against his hard member. She massaged and stroked him through his breeches until he cursed deeply. He unbuttoned the front and his member sprang free.

Olivia sat back to look at it. Far larger than she expected, it stood straight up pointing toward the sky.

She didn't think it prudent to say so, but it was a bit odd-looking as well. She had imagined it a fair number of times and it had looked nothing like this.

He started to unbutton the front of her gown. "I have wanted to undo these buttons since I first met you."

She looked down at his hands. "Really? My mother says I look like a spinster."

"Hmm. Well, I've never wanted to undress a spinster before. It's quite erotic."

Olivia leaned closer to unbutton his vest. "I've never sat atop an exposed man before. I dare say that's quite erotic."

She leaned over until his member prodded her. "I think I'd like it more if we were both completely naked."

"That can be arranged," he said, and flipped her on to her back, settling himself between her legs.

He ran his hands up her thighs, under her dress, pushing it up to her waist. He stared down at her, fingering her curls. He grinned wickedly at her. "You're enjoying this, aren't you? I can see you glistening already."

"Nathaniel!"

He chuckled, leaning over to kiss her. His erection probed her and she held her breath, aching for him. His tongue flicked against her lips, entering slowly to dance with hers. He tasted warm, moist.

"Wrap your legs around my waist."

As she did, the head of his member slid into her. She gasped, gripping his hair.

He stilled, watching her. Then he slowly began to move in a rhythmic pumping that opened her further, his member sliding deeper into her.

Their breaths came in short huffs, Olivia wondering if this was pain or pleasure. He was unbearably large.

Nathaniel stopped for a moment, allowing her to relax, and she breathed deeply.

He murmured, "I've never introduced a virgin before. You are so very, very tight."

She huffed. "I think, sir, the fault lies with you. You seem quite large. Enormous."

Nathaniel raised to his elbows, his eyes twinkling wickedly. "That wasn't a complaint, Olivia. I'm enjoying this far more than I should."

"Oh."

He kissed her deeply and began moving again until, finally, he slid resistance-free to her core, his member sheathed completely.

He held still, his breathing heavy. "Did I hurt you?"

She shook her head, unable to speak. She had never been so close to anyone in her life. He was a part of her; indeed, she wondered if he always would be. She would never forget this moment. Never forget how warm and excited she felt.

Olivia wiggled beneath him, feeling minute movements inside her, and he groaned.

"Dear God, this is going to be a

very short lesson."

"Are you hurt, Nathaniel?"

He slid out of her and she couldn't hide her moue of disappointment. Was that it?

He slid in again, surprising her.

"Olivia. . . I can't. . . I swear. . ."

He began pumping harder, Olivia gripping his arms. A warm tingle spread through her body. She gasped, trying to get air into her lungs. Nathaniel gave a final lunge, groaned, and quickly pulled completely out.

His head fell to her breast and he gulped air in. Olivia stared at the stars. She felt quite warm and oddly bereft now that he was no longer inside her, although she could see that the experience had meant far more to Nathaniel than to her. She could see now why he wouldn't be paid.

"I'm sorry, Olivia."

He rolled to lay beside her, his hand resting on her abdomen.

"That's quite all right. I would

have preferred to have seen you naked, but it was quite wonderful anyway."

He stared at her. "That wasn't quite what I meant."

He fingered her curls, tickling her. His fingers slowly moved lower and a *frisson* moved through her. He touched her, slowly rubbing, the friction sending tingles through her.

"I'm getting warm again, Nathaniel."

He kissed her hard, his tongue pumping into her mouth, mimicking his earlier actions. "Good."

Olivia held her breath. "Oh! Nathaniel!"

"Come for me, Olivia."

Her body suddenly went rigid, his fingers rubbing faster and harder, and every muscle in her body clenched as she exploded in a pulsing wave of heat. Her toes curled and she whimpered as her innermost muscles contracted quickly.

She lay back in a stupor, staring at the night sky.

Finally Nathaniel said, "I don't think I'll be able to teach you everything you wish to learn in one night, Olivia."

She was too relaxed to turn her head but agreed with him. "Indeed, Nathaniel. The art of seduction will take some studying."

"It seems we are almost always in agreement, my dear."

"Almost."

He rolled to his knees, positioning himself between her knees.

Olivia looked at him in surprise. "Again?"

"Unless you object?"

She stretched beneath him and slowly smiled. "I don't object, but perhaps you can remove your boots?"

"Indeed."

Olivia awoke to sunlight streaming through her window, the songs of birds serenading her, and the smell of hot sausages tantalizing her.

She stretched lazily, smiling to herself.

What a glorious morning.

Her mother knocked on the door, entreating her to get up. "What if your Mr. Jenkins comes this morning, Livvy? I don't want to have to tell him you are still abed."

Olivia doubted that would shock him at all.

"I'm up, Mama. I'll be down presently."

She bounded out of bed, nearly falling to the floor, and groaned as all the muscles in her lower extremities protested. Dear heaven, she was sore!

She winced as she took another step and silently berated herself. How was she supposed to comport herself in front of her parents when it felt like she had been thoroughly used! How was she supposed to walk down the confounded stairs without killing herself!

No one had ever mentioned this little side effect, thank you very much. She expected her nether regions to be a bit sore, which they were, but not nearly as sore as her backside. Perhaps that was from the hard deck.

Her next lesson would need to be on something a bit softer.

Olivia dressed slowly, stretching her abused muscles, and praying her parents would not know by looking at her that she was no longer a virgin spinster aunt.

She was a ruined spinster aunt, thank you very much.

The stairs gave her pause. She held firm to the rod, groaning with each step, thankful no one could see her.

Her mother and father were already sitting at the table and eating when she arrived. Her appetite ravenous, she filled her plate, and stiffly sat in her chair.

Her mother glanced at her. "Are you ill, Olivia? I hope you haven't caught a cold. A man's attention is very fragile and now would be a bad time to lose Mr. Jenkins' interest."

Olivia tucked into her eggs. "I am not ill. I fell asleep in my chair last night and am a bit stiff."

Her father frowned over his spectacles. "Shall I send Haskins out with you, my dear? I know you do not like company, but this is not the country. Even if you are on the roof."

"No, Papa. I shan't be falling asleep again, trust me."

Her mother sighed. "What Mr. Jenkins would say about your nocturnal tendencies, I know not." She pointed her fork at her daughter and shook it. "You are not a normal girl, Olivia."

Olivia bit back a laugh. "I rather think he knows that, Mama. I don't try to hide it."

"Well, don't tell him that we let you outside at night alone. I shudder to think the scandal that would bring. Better if he finds out after the wedding."

Seven

It had been almost a se'nnight since Nathaniel had come to her that night and Olivia was feeling quite a bit restless. Anxious. Impatient.

Oh, she saw him nearly every day. He came calling regularly, and danced with her repeatedly, and everyone in the family called him her Mr. Jenkins.

She refused to be seen anywhere else in public with him and had tried to limit one dance per night with him, but she could hardly refuse him a second one, especially as he asked when she was surrounded by her family.

She had explained that she was trying to be discreet to protect his reputation but he had merely laughed. She couldn't help but feel a tiny bit excited and alarmed with his public attentions.

But if her Mr. Jenkins did not commit to a private rendezvous soon she was going to start screaming.

Olivia took a deep breath and smiled at Mary. She now realized why Nathaniel had been cautious in introducing her to the *acte d'amour*. No longer was she content with dances and kisses. She wanted more. Needed more. No wonder young women were kept oblivious to the marital act until safely married. It would not do at all to have young women chasing after men, knocking them to the ground and having their wicked way with them.

She saw Nathaniel enter the room and tried not to run to him like some lovesick ninny. She smiled pleasantly when he caught her eye and ignored her rapidly beating heart as he made his way to them.

"Mrs. Eliot, Miss Blakesley."

"Mr. Jenkins."

"Would you have the next dance free?"

Olivia scowled at him. "Really, Na– Mr. Jenkins. You just can't come dance with me as soon as you walk in the door. Wander around a bit, mingle. You are giving the gossips too much to work with."

Mary hid a laugh behind her fan. "Are you often scolded by the women you seek out, Mr. Jenkins? I'm surprised you take it so well."

He smiled. "I don't take it to heart, Mrs. Eliot. She insists on preserving my bachelor reputation despite my decided lack of enjoyment in it. If it weren't for how sweetly she welcomes my company when she is not worrying what others think, I would leave her be."

"My sister? Worrying about what others think? Sweet?"

Mary looked at Olivia and smiled so happily that Olivia shuddered. Her mother would take one look at Mary and assume Nathaniel had proposed right then and there.

Mary sighed. "Oh, Olivia."

Olivia turned away from her. "Oh, all right. Let's go dance."

Nathaniel chuckled, taking her hand in his.

"Nathaniel, you are all but declaring your intentions with this tomfoolery. My family will be stricken when nothing comes of it."

"Perhaps something will come of it."

Her face darkened with anger. "You and I both know that isn't true. We have an agreement. You are not holding up your end."

"I thought part of it was wooing and winning."

"You've wooed, you've won. Now stop it."

"I wonder why I don't feel as if

I've won."

Olivia muttered, "It is because you have not been fulfilling all your contractual obligations."

A diabolical smile lit his face and Olivia nearly tripped over her own foot.

"Do you feel as if I have been ignoring a certain aspect of your education, Olivia?"

She chose to ignore him rather than risk looking a besotted fool and was taken completely by surprise when her mouth opened of its own volition and hissed, "A week!"

"It has seemed like an eternity to me."

She felt slightly mollified. "Then why have you not come?"

"It was to give you time, Olivia. You were quite sore after."

"True, but that went away quickly."

"And then it was because I wanted to visit you."

She thought for a moment. "You

didn't visit because you wanted to visit?"

"It does sound silly when you say it, but I do not like my passions to get out of control."

"Ah. Yes." She smiled. "I do turn most of the men around me into ravenous beasts."

"You make one out of me."

She laughed. "I don't believe you but it is a pretty excuse."

"It is the truth but if you won't believe it then let's move on from excuses and on to plans."

Her stomach flopped. "Plans? Have you resumed control of your beast then?"

He shook his head. "I am afraid he will be in control for quite some time. I no longer care."

"Well then, when shall I expect your ravenous beast?" And why, oh why, was that thought so titillating? Nathaniel so in passion that he lost all control?

"Perhaps tonight I can rein him in enough to not scare you."

"Please don't on my account. I am slightly interested in meeting him."

Nathaniel coughed, nearly missing the next step. "Dear God."

And Miss Olivia Blakesley, for the first time in her life, giggled.

Mr. Nathaniel Jenkins had come to the conclusion this past torturous week that Olivia Blakesley was the woman he had been waiting to marry. He had never met a woman who intrigued him more. Who could surprise him with her thoughts and conclusions. Who tormented him with her diabolical choice of dress.

He was not made to marry any young girl who thought the color orange was sophisticated. He preferred somber colors. He preferred high necks, not floating cleavage. He preferred conversation and debate. He preferred Olivia.

He wanted to marry her. They

were perfect for each other. He did not in the least fear that she would have nothing to do with her day, her life, than coddle him or want him to coddle her. She had interests. Even better, she had interests that would not cost him an obscene amount of money.

Of course, he would marry her even if she wanted him to build an observatory, but he considered that highly unlikely.

She was passionate. Far more passionate than he had expected from any gently bred lady of the *ton.*

She was far more curious than any lady of the *ton.* He would need to keep her satiated, intrigued. He wouldn't want her trying to buy other men.

A dark moment passed while he wondered if she would proposition some young buck if Nathaniel did not keep her satisfied. He shook his head. She had resorted to that out of desperation, and she was at least twenty-seven. It wasn't as if she had begun propositioning strange men as soon as she'd entered society.

His previous vision of a cold, duty-filled marriage died around her. No sneaking off to a mistress for love, or to his club for thought-filled conversation. He could easily imagine years of happiness tucked away in the country arguing and laughing.

Yes, Olivia was perfect. And thankfully, already his.

They were meant to be.

This time Olivia had provided the blanket, and she paced beside it waiting for him. She had waited every night for a week, on the chance that he might come. She had felt like a silly ninny every night when he hadn't. If it weren't for his attentions during the daylight hours, she would have assumed he'd had his pleasure and was done with her. Truthfully, he had performed his obligations. They should end the whole thing.

But she didn't want to.

When he'd told her starting a physical relationship changed things, she'd thought he'd been exaggerating. Perhaps it was simply because it was new to her, but she found herself thinking of him all day long. When he was close and she could smell him, she often thought she might faint from longing. It was embarrassing! She, of all people. Felled by passion.

Olivia exhaled loudly when he found her. He had come. The night was cool and she was glad she did not have to wait long for him, for his heat.

Nathaniel bent to one knee, bringing a bouquet of flowers from behind his back.

Olivia took a step back. "What are you doing?"

"I'm asking you to marry me."

"Oh, Nathaniel. I can't marry

you."

Nathaniel stared. "Pardon? Have you become engaged to someone else while I wasn't looking?"

Olivia frowned. "Of course not. But you are simply feeling guilty for taking my. . ."

". . .maidenhead?"

"My innocence."

"As you said before, Olivia, you were not an innocent. Inexperienced, and I rectified that, but you were definitely not an innocent."

True. But she couldn't help feeling that this was a mistake and blamed it on his honor. He had ruined her for marriage, she was sure he thought so, and proposed to her out of guilt.

"Nathaniel. I can't marry you."

"Why not? We are eminently suited for each other."

"I would make you a terrible wife. I have been alone for too long."

Nathaniel shook his head.

"Yes, I have. Not even you would let me sneak outside every clear night."

"Well–"

"And what about children? I'm not sure I'm mother material. I don't like being constantly distracted."

"Olivia–"

"I do like being an aunt, it's true. But I get to go home at the end of the day. When they stub their little toes, it's not me they go running to."

"Olivia, I hate to mention this but we have been intimate. You may already be pregnant."

Olivia stared at him indignantly. "I thought you had taken care of that!"

Nathaniel shrugged. "There is always the possibility."

She sat down in silence, considering. Finally, she shook her head. "I don't think so."

"And you're right, I wouldn't let you sneak outside every clear night. It's too dangerous and I can't believe your father allows it."

"I told you."

"But I would build you a tower. An observatory that you could escape to but would be safe."

She stared at him, torn between laughter at the idea and amazement. Had he considered this already?

"An observatory?"

"With your easels out there already– a chair, blankets. You could simply slip up there and I wouldn't worry." He laughed. "I was just congratulating myself on choosing an inexpensive wife."

Olivia shook her head. "It wouldn't be the same."

"It would be better."

"I like helping my father with the estate. Truthfully, he hasn't cared for the books in nearly five years."

"I don't see why you would have to stop doing that. Indeed, I would enjoy input from you about my estates."

She shook her head. "I am as free as any woman could ever be. My life is exactly as I want it."

He took her hand. "When I am with you, my future does not seem so dark. When I am with you, life is colorful and wonderful. Can you not say the same?"

She whispered sadly, "Nathaniel. . ."

He let go of her hand. "Think on it, Olivia. We are perfect for each other."

She shook her head. "It's impossible. Perhaps we could go on like this."

Nathaniel rose, taking a step back. "Perhaps not. One day we will both tire of sneaking around." He pointed at the hard deck. "We will tire of bruised backsides. We will tire of having to separate at the end of the day."

Olivia said nothing, merely watched him with sad eyes.

He turned to leave and she rose from her chair quickly. "Will you not stay tonight?"

He shook his head. "I came offering you the stars and all you want is the moon. I will not settle for less, Olivia."

Eight

Nathaniel found his mother at home the next morning. He threw himself into a chair, flopping into a boneless heap.

"Good morning, Nathaniel."

"Mother. Prepare yourself; I'm getting married."

"Hallelujah. I assume to Miss Blakesley?"

"You assume correctly. However, there is a small problem."

His mother said, "And you've come to me to fix it? How odd. Are you feeling quite well, dear?"

"No. I have a recalcitrant bride-to-be who will not listen to me at all."

"Hmm. You've picked well for yourself. I'd hate for you to be saddled with a woman who ran to do your bidding."

Nathaniel tipped his head. "Thank you. Now will you help me?"

"Of course. A woman always needs more grandchildren."

Nathaniel muttered under his breath. Where the idea came from that the female was the weaker sex, he had no idea. They always did exactly what they wished.

Anne said, "First, I must make sure that the lady in question does want to marry you. I would hate to coerce Miss Blakesley into marrying an ogre if she didn't love you."

"Thank you again, Mother. Why don't I ask Barters to stab me in the back as well."

"Your valet would never do such a thing, even if you begged. Blood is quite awful to get out of cloth." She skewered her son with *the look*.

"Why does Miss Blakesley refuse your hand?"

"I don't know. Yes, I do. Because she has had too much freedom in the past. Too much time to think. She should have been married ages ago. She says she would make me a terrible wife."

"Hmm. Have you considered that she may not love you, Nathaniel? I do not mean to be cruel, but perhaps she was being tactful."

"Olivia? Tactful? She's never heard the word. If she didn't want to marry me she would have come right out and told me I was an under-educated toad." He sighed. "She came damned close to tears when she refused me. She is simply being stubborn."

She nodded, satisfied. "I shall call on a few ladies. How do they say it in the militia? I will gather my forces. It is a mother's duty to see her children married."

Anne held her hand out to Nathaniel and he rose to his feet

swiftly.

She said, "Shall we plan on an autumn wedding?"

"I would prefer summer. Perhaps I'll apply for a special license. Or carry her off to Gretna Green. I'll need some rope and a gag."

She shook her head. "No, Nathaniel. I only have two children and I will have full weddings for the both of you. Leave Olivia to me."

"Thank you, Mother. I knew I could count on you."

"Of course, my dear. That's what mothers are for."

"Mrs. Anne Jenkins is here to see you, Ma'am."

Mrs. Blakesley nervously ran her fingers over her cap and fingered her *fichu*. "Anne Jenkins? Send her in, send her in. Oh, dear!"

What in the world was Mrs. Jenkins doing over here at this hour?

The housekeeper escorted Mrs. Jenkins in and Mrs. Blakesley rose. "Mrs. Jenkins."

"Mrs. Blakesley. I do apologize for intruding at this hour, but I fear it is an emergency."

"Of course, of course. Sit down, please."

"Thank you." Mrs. Jenkins sat demurely, barely glancing at the arrangement of the room and offering no courtesies. "Mrs. Blakesley, you must be aware of the attachment between our children."

Mrs. Blakesley nodded. Then her eyes widened and her hand flew to her chest. "Tell me they have not run off to Gretna Green, Mrs. Jenkins! Oh, the scandal!"

"They have not run off to Gretna Green."

"Oh. Then, pray tell, what is the emergency?"

"Perhaps I spoke in haste. However, there is a matter that must needs be drawn to our attention. It is our duty to see our children married fortuitously, happily, and if at all possible, before our deaths. You must agree with me, Mrs. Blakesley."

Mrs. Blakesley held her breath, trying to dampen her growing anger. "I do quite agree with you, Mrs. Jenkins. And I find the match to be fortuitous and happy for both sides."

"As do I. Which is why we must act together to marry them off."

Mrs. Blakesley blinked. "Pardon me, Mrs. Jenkins. For a moment there I thought you had come to run my daughter off."

"Oh, dear. Of course not. I find the match perfectly acceptable. Miss Blakesley is not as young as some girls these days, but I find that suits my son better. He would never be happy with a silly girl. The matter I wish to bring to your attention is the fact that my son has already proposed to Miss Blakesley."

Mrs. Blakesley fluttered her handkerchief and bit back a squeal. "All six of my daughters married! Oh, Mrs. Jenkins, this is not an emergency!"

"She refused him."

"Pardon?"

"Miss Blakesley turned him down."

Mrs. Blakesley's eyebrows drew together and she leaned back heavily in her chair. "My daughter has refused the only marriage proposal she will ever receive?"

Mrs. Jenkins nodded.

Mrs. Blakesley folded her hands carefully in her lap. "I understand the emergency now, Mrs. Jenkins."

"Thank you. We both have children who remain unmarried far longer than one would wish. I intend to rectify that."

"Indeed. I shall help."

"Olivia."

"Mama? What is the matter?"

"I was visited by Mrs. Jenkins today."

Olivia looked down at her painting, mentally cursing herself. She should have expected this. Nathaniel was not the sort to give up easily.

"I was not aware you knew Mrs. Jenkins."

"Of course we've met, Olivia. Our children were spending quite a bit of time together. In fact, some people would have been expecting an announcement soon."

Olivia sighed. Whatever Mrs. Jenkins had told her mother, and Olivia was more than a little worried about that, it wasn't good. She could tell by the calm, monotonous voice.

"An announcement seems a bit premature to me. But perhaps tongues start to wag as soon as a man asks for a dance."

Her mother bent down until her nose nearly touched Olivia's cheek. "It wouldn't have been premature if you had accepted his proposal."

"Ah. That was a bit quick. I hadn't expected you to hear of that quite yet." Or Mrs. Jenkins. Had Nathaniel told her? Everything?

Mrs. Blakesley walked to an empty stool and dragged it across the room, positioning it beside Olivia. She smiled stiffly and sat.

"I had thought Mr. Jenkins to have the approval of your brothers. Have you discovered some serious flaw in his character?"

Olivia muttered, "Brothers-in-law, Mother. You of all people should know I have no blood brothers." Her mother's forced *bonhomie* was more frightening than her anger.

Mrs. Blakesley ignored her. "Perhaps he has a gambling addiction?"

"I doubt it."

"He lost his temper and frightened you?"

"Mr. Jenkins? Please, Mother. He's certainly lost his patience with me, but never his temper."

Her mother watched her for a moment, then turned to stare out the window.

"He's kissed you, hasn't he?"

Olivia couldn't stop the blush from blossoming across her cheeks. She ducked her head, hoping her hair blocked her mother's view.

"Oh, Olivia. He has!" She cleared her throat. "A man's passions are not to be feared, Livvy."

Olivia's mouth dropped open and she stared at her mother in horror. "Moth–"

"No, it was not proper for him to kiss you, but not entirely unexpected. He has scared you."

Olivia placed her paintbrush gently on the easel. Perhaps she could tiptoe out of the room and drown herself?

Her mother continued. "A man's urges are sometimes wild and uncontrollable, Livvy. But a wife's duty is not always a duty. It is possible to. . . to enjoy a husband's embrace."

Oh, dear God. "Mother, please! There is no need, really. Mr. Jenkins did not scare me!"

Her mother breathed a sigh of relief. "Good, good. Because there really is nothing to fear."

Olivia turned to her mother and grabbed her hands, hoping to forestall any more embarrassing reassurances. "He did not scare me, Mother. And if I were to marry, I would be quite lucky to have him as a husband. But I am not wifely material. I would be awful! I do as I please and neither you nor Papa has ever been able to make me do otherwise. That is not a good quality for a wife. You must admit that."

Her mother looked torn between a stubborn refusal to admit the truth and the dashed hopes of seeing all her daughters happily married.

Olivia squeezed her hands. "I respect Mr. Jenkins far too much to saddle him with me for a wife."

"Perhaps you do not respect him enough to let him decide what he wants in a wife."

Olivia stood, stowing her paints and brushes quickly. "He shouldn't want me. I should never have accosted him. He is a good man, a decent man, an honorable man! And I, dear mother, am an idiot. I should have seen this."

"Seen what? That a good, decent man would want to marry you? Of course he would! You have many good qualities to offer a husband."

"Oh, yes? Do you think he would want me to take over the books for him? I shall certainly offer my services, but that does not mean he should marry me. I am what I am, Mother. A spinster extraordinaire."

"Olivia Blakesley! Do not use that foul word in this household!"

"It is not a foul word. And just because you attack anyone who utters it doesn't change the fact. Can you not see what I am, who I am? Nothing! Nobody! Five daughters married is enough! I am happy! I want nothing more! I do not want Mr. Nathaniel Jenkins!"

Nine

Nathaniel was unsurprised when his sister burst into his library. He'd expected her much earlier.

"Nathaniel."

"Diana. How are you?"

"Good. Hold him, won't you?" She thrust Nathaniel's latest nephew into his arms. "He will not be put down and insists on crying in my ear."

Nathaniel held his nephew expertly, jiggling the boy and making faces until he stopped his wailing. "What a mean mama you have, Jacob. Doesn't she know that crying is simply your way of saying you want a biscuit?"

"Oh, Mama knows it. His fondness for biscuits is why my arms are about ready to fall off." She eyed him. "It looks like children are in your future after all, hmm?"

"If Mother has anything to say about it."

Diana said, "She always does. She approves of the girl, at least. Not the usual shrinking violet and not a gold-digger."

"No. Olivia is quite unique."

"And older? I always thought an older girl would do better for you."

Nathaniel said, "Yes, amazing how everyone comes to that conclusion after I've already found her."

"Oh, shush. When am I to meet her?"

Nathaniel gratefully accepted a biscuit from his butler, offering it to a suddenly alert Jacob.

"That's better, hmm little one?"

Diana eyed her youngest as he

munched happily. "Only if you're not the one who has to carry him all day."

"Where's the nanny?"

"Left. He's gone through four already. I've started offering three days off with pay to keep them a little longer. You didn't answer my question."

Nathaniel grinned at her. "No? Well, I expect Mother has already told you."

"That she won't marry you? Have you mentioned your sizable fortune?"

"Thank you, Diana. I'm sure that will solve everything."

She shrugged. "If the girl is over twenty-five, I don't see what she is waiting for. Perhaps she is simply worried about the business end of marriage."

"I'm not sure what she's worried about."

"Mother says she cried when she refused you."

He shook his head. "Nearly cried.

Was there anything Mother didn't tell you?"

"She didn't tell me when I could meet her."

"I believe she is going to the Mayes affair tonight."

"Oh, really? What extraordinarily good luck."

"Don't scare her off, Diana."

She gave a ladylike snort. "I assume you have not met her sisters. She has five, did you know? They can all hold their own quite well. The eldest came out the same year as I. I had thought her quite the original but each sister seems to surpass the others one way or another. I doubt Miss Olivia Blakesley would even blink at anything I said."

"Nevertheless, I want her to join the family, not run screaming from it."

Diana smiled. "She's not met Mother, then? Perhaps Miss Blakesley is refusing because she is unsure of your sincerity. She's not met any of your relations, after all."

Nathaniel wiped biscuit crumbs from his knee and offered another to Jacob. "I fear she will find out all too soon that I was showing her my fondest respect by keeping my relations from her."

"I'll endeavor not to overwhelm her, but I really don't think you need to worry. I fully expect Miss Blakesley to be able to hold her own against me or Mother." She picked Jacob up, preparing to depart, and raised an eyebrow at her brother. "She is, after all, holding her own against you."

He grimaced, rising and kissing her cheek. "It is my greatest character fault– finding sweet, biddable women utterly boring."

She laughed. "Then you should be grateful you have none in your life. Until tonight brother, dear."

Mary burst into Olivia's room, the bedchamber key dangling from her finger. "A little trick I learned from you."

Olivia glared at her. "Go away. That door was locked for a reason."

"Yes, I know. So you could mope about. *Oh, poor me. I have been proposed to– the horror of it all. However will I survive!*"

"Rot you, Mary. You don't have Mother harassing you into an unsuitable marriage."

Mary sat on the bed. "Oh. So you don't love him then? Forgive us. We all thought you had formed quite the attachment. I suspect he thought it as well." She watched Olivia intently. "Tell me you don't love him."

"I don't love him. I should have cut it off but he is remarkably persistent."

"And you are quite the accomplished liar. You should be treading the boards."

"Must I fall in love with the first gentleman who comes calling?"

"I have never seen you happier. I

have never seen a connection between two people as I see with you. It is as if you've known each other for years, grew up with each other." She stood, taking Olivia's hand. "Olivia. He is who you have been waiting for. Why do you say no?"

Olivia whispered, "I tricked him. He is infatuated only. One day he will wake up and realize his mistake."

Mary hugged her, squeezing hard. "You're a ninny."

Olivia tried to pull away, but Mary held fast. "He is not a boy, he is a grown man. I would expect he is remarkably hard to trick."

"Then how do you explain this madness, hmm?"

Mary laughed. "He loves you, you silly twit!"

She shook her head. "We must disagree."

"Let's go ask him."

Olivia reared back in horror. "What!"

"I'm sure he'll be at the Mayes' tonight. We'll ask him why he insisted on doing something so foolish as proposing to you."

"You have gone mad."

"I don't think I'm the mad one in this room."

Olivia pointed her finger at Mary. "Do not dare embarrass me by asking him *anything.*"

"Oh, do you care then what he thinks of you and your family? Intriguing."

"Mary, promise me."

Mary shrugged, heading toward the door. "You'll have to try and keep me from him this evening. And Rufus." She laughed. "That would be even worse, don't you think?"

Olivia sat unseeing on the bed, imagining Mary and Rufus accosting Nathaniel and demanding his declaration of love. She whispered, "You are horrific."

Mary stopped at the door. "I would do anything to secure the future happiness of my favorite sister. Anything at all."

"I thought you would be the one person I could count on to be on my side."

"Perhaps you should examine why I am not. Perhaps you are in the wrong, Olivia." She waved. "See you tonight, my dear."

Olivia lay back on the bed. For the first time in her life she felt outmatched by her family and did not in the slightest enjoy the experience.

"A Mr. Edward Blakesley to see you, sir."

Nathaniel sat back unexpectedly. He had not spoken to her father about his intentions, mainly because he wasn't certain Olivia would ever accept him.

"Show him in please."

Her father entered the study dressed as the country gentleman he was. His spectacles perched on his nose, his greying hair clipped short. Olivia took after him with her willowy frame.

Mr. Blakesley reminded him of his own father. Quiet, calm, and ruled by the women in his life. Nathaniel's mother and sister had run his childhood home and he could see a similar situation with Mr. Blakesley. He felt a twinge of camaraderie for another man surrounded by forceful women.

Mr. Blakesley smiled and took the seat Nathaniel offered. "Thank you, m'boy. Once a man becomes a grandfather it seems his energy is sucked away."

"My father said something similar when my oldest nephew was born."

"It reminds us how far away our own childhood was." Mr. Blakesley cleared his throat. "I understand you have been pursuing my daughter."

"Yes, sir. I'm sorry I have not spoken with you, but considering she hasn't accepted I thought it prudent to wait."

Mr. Blakesley chuckled. "Yes. That is what I came to speak to you about. I thought I'd warn you that once Olivia gets an idea in her head, it is notoriously difficult to get out. You have an uphill battle, I'm afraid."

"I've noticed she does forge her own path."

"That is certainly one way of putting it. I'm the father of six girls, Mr. Jenkins. They each have their own personalities and traits, it seems like from birth. I love them all dearly. But I must confess that Olivia has always had a special place in my heart. There are not many men who know exactly what they do and do not want, and go after it with single-minded abandon the way she does. It has turned my hair grey and given her mother apoplexy on many occasions."

Nathaniel smiled. "I can certainly believe that, sir."

"And I would not want anyone to change that about her."

"No, sir."

Mr. Blakesley stared at him, appraising him. Finally he nodded. "However, none of us are infallible. She has been wrong before and I think she is wrong this time. Olivia has never been so happy and I credit that to you. You seem to understand her and that is something we should all be so lucky to find."

He stood to his feet, waving Nathaniel down. "I will give you a tip, m'boy. Force will only make her dig her heels in deeper. But she will listen and gather evidence, and when she has enough proof, she will change her opinion. Don't give up. Have patience." Mr. Blakesley winked. "You'll need plenty of it."

Ten

The Mayes' Ball was crowded and merry; everyone was laughing and being overly happy. Olivia could not keep a scowl off her face. She had never been in a worse temper. Her head pounded with every step she took and every beat of the music. Mary was attached to her like a limpet on a rock and her mother watched her like a hawk watching a mouse. What were they expecting her to do? Make a run for it through the garden?

She was here to keep *them* from confronting Nathaniel!

She had been threatened and

bullied into coming and now they acted as if she was their prisoner. It was nearly too much to bear.

Not to mention she had not seen Nathaniel for days, not since he had lost his mind and proposed to her. Would he even be here? If he came, would he acknowledge her? Would she acknowledge him?

"Miss Blakesley?"

Olivia turned to find an elegantly dressed woman she had never met before.

"Very shocking, I know– we have not been introduced– but really, I can't stand to wait on such niceties. I have a few words I'd like to say to you."

"Perhaps a few of those words would be your name?"

Diana smiled. "I told Nathaniel I could not run you off. I am Diana Cracraft, his sister." She nodded at Mary, though kept her focus on Olivia. Mary did not even try to hide her glee-filled smile.

Olivia sighed. "Oh. Have you

come to harass me into marrying your brother?"

"Of course I have. He seems quite taken with you despite your rejection and I wanted to see why."

"I really don't know why he sees fit to tell everyone I refused him. I would think most men would keep that to themselves."

"Ah well, my brother is not like most men, is he? Besides, he expects to win you eventually."

Diana stared at Olivia, as if willing her to divulge her innermost secrets. Olivia stared back, the silence lengthening, until finally Diana conceded defeat, smiling slightly.

"No, no. Don't tell me why you've refused. That is, apparently, between you and my brother. I will simply warn you. If you have good reason not to accept Nathaniel's hand, then steer clear of him. I will not have his heart broken– he is a most sensitive man– and he deserves to marry and have children. Soon."

Olivia inhaled deeply. "Steer clear of Nathaniel? So says the sister who has accosted me."

Diana laughed. "And if you don't have good reason, then stop playing with him and welcome to the family. I assure you Mother and I are not so formidable once you get to know us."

Diana patted her hand, then waved to a friend through the crowd. "Ah, there is Emily Mayes. I really must tell her to stop wearing that dreadful feather in her hair. I'll come and have a chat sometime this week, yes? Until then, Miss Blakesley."

Olivia watched as Nathaniel's sister navigated the crowds, then surreptitiously patted her dress and hair. She felt as if a very strong wind had blown through.

No wonder he seemed to have a limitless supply of patience and fortitude. His sister had bred it into him. Olivia shuddered at the thought of meeting his mother. Did the man have to tell all his relations?

Out of the corner of her eye, she saw him. She turned, glaring, and her temper sparked.

"Let go of my arm this instant, Mary. There is someone I wish to yell at."

Mary turned to look. "Shall I come with you?"

"No, I don't want you anywhere near him."

Mary laughed and let go of her arm. "Say hello from Rufus and me. I think I will go contrive an introduction to his sister. She seemed an interesting sort."

Olivia bit back her scream and made good on her escape, targeting Nathaniel through the crowd like a dog on a fox. He met her halfway.

"Olivia, you look lovely."

"Nathaniel, call off your family."

He took her arm and they began to circulate around the fringe of the dance floor.

"Are you being hounded, my dear?"

"As you well know. Your mother has colluded with my mother, your sister accosted me just moments ago, my family will not give me a moments peace. It is all your fault."

"I don't think you can lay your family's attentions on my shoulders, although I will accept that my mother and sister can be quite fearsome."

"It *is* your fault. If you had not told all and sundry that you had proposed, I would not be the subject of my family's machinations. If any of them approach you, you must make a hasty exit; I fear a few of them have gone quite mad."

He laughed. "My dear, you do know that all of this would stop if you would simply say yes."

"That was not our agreement."

He sighed loudly. "I do not know how to make this more plain, Olivia. I wish to make a new agreement."

She sniffed. "Our old agreement was working just fine."

"Not for me."

"This is really quite vexing. You do know that normally it is the woman who cannot get marriage out of her mind and the gentleman who wants nothing more than some fun. I really was not expecting this scenario."

Nathaniel stopped suddenly. "Are you saying, my dear, that I am good enough for some fun but not good enough for marriage?"

She looked at him reproachfully. "Of course that is not what I am saying. Don't be silly."

"I am trying to understand. You do not wish to marry me, yet you seem quite happy to have my company. Is it the idea of marriage to me or the idea of marriage at all that you object to?"

She squeezed his arm. "Oh, Nathaniel. If I were to marry, I think you are the only man I would ever risk it for. But I do not think I will agree with marriage at all. I refuse in order to save us a great deal of torment."

He was silent a moment, thinking. "Then I can only see two ways out of our current predicament."

She looked at him suspiciously. "And they are?"

"One, we continue to abide by our original agreement while I try to encourage you to accept a new agreement."

"And the other?"

"We say goodbye, end all public and private interactions, and never see each other again."

Olivia's stomach knotted, her heart ached. She whispered, "That would probably be for the best. It is the ending we agreed upon; it will happen eventually."

"If you have your way, yes."

"I do not like that option at all."

Nathaniel looked down at her. "Neither do I. I much prefer to live with the hope that one day I can talk you into accepting my outrageous proposal."

"Those are my only options, then? Live with constant harassment or never see you again?"

"That is how it appears to me."

She eyed him critically. "I am not at all sure you are worth the aggravation."

He deposited her to Mary and Rufus, bowing. "Then I must prove that I am."

Nathaniel joined his mother and sister on a settee away from the dancing.

His sister raised an eyebrow. "I assume there is no change in her answer?"

He nodded.

"Are you quite sure she is worth the effort? Perhaps she has a very good reason for not wanting to marry you."

"It is not me she objects to but marriage in general. I think she quite likes me despite her reservations."

"And you like her?"

He smiled. "She constantly surprises me, makes me laugh, challenges me." He laughed. "I quite expected that whoever I proposed to would fall over dead with gratitude. I would win her hand in marriage but have no desire to win her heart. Olivia is the complete opposite. I have her heart but she refuses my hand. It is a most enjoyable skirmish."

"You are a very strange fellow."

"I wanted a different kind of girl. There's no one more different than Olivia; her refusal only proves that."

His mother smiled. "You are so much like your father. I'm afraid he had to ask me more than once as well." She laughed. "Stubborn women do very well in this family. I shall pay her a visit."

Diana nodded. "Shall I come, too?

"Let's keep you in the reserves, darling. This may be a protracted battle."

Nathaniel smiled. "Don't be put out, Diana. I fully expect that Olivia will need constant irritation."

A few mornings later, Olivia was sitting with her mother when the housekeeper announced a visitor.

"Mrs. Anne Jenkins is here, ma'am."

"Thank you, Hill."

Olivia jumped to her feet and turned to her mother reproachfully. "Oh, Mother."

"You sit down, Olivia."

Mrs. Jenkins entered the cozy room, smiling at Mrs. Blakesley. "Mrs. Blakesley, how are you this morning?"

"In fine spirits, thank you. Have you met my daughter Olivia?"

"Miss Blakesley."

"Mrs. Jenkins."

Mrs. Jenkins settled herself on the sofa, accepting a cup of tea. "So, Miss Blakesley. I hear you have refused my son's offer of marriage."

Olivia sighed. "Yes, Mrs. Jenkins."

"And why is that? He is my son, and therefore I am biased of course, but I cannot think why anyone would refuse him."

Olivia heard the unspoken– *especially by an old spinster like you.*

She said, "I must assume, since he told you I wouldn't marry him, why as well."

Mrs. Jenkins waved that suggestion away. "He's a man, what would he know about a woman's reluctance to marry."

Olivia sat down and Mrs. Jenkins leaned forward to pat her hand. "Are you surprised that I understand? Every woman must wonder about the man she is marrying. Every woman must wonder how her life will change."

Olivia turned to her mother. "Were you apprehensive when you married Papa?"

Mrs. Blakesley patted her other hand. "Of course I was, Olivia. I left my family to live with a man I'd spoken to a handful of times. It is upsetting at the best of times. My father had made all of my decisions before then, I knew what to expect, and suddenly another man was to make those decisions. I married a good man but there is a relearning period no matter how good."

Mrs. Jenkins said, "My son is a good man. Although I wonder if you will have the same worries and expectations your mother and I did. You are older, and with that comes a certain independence of spirit. I doubt if you will let my son make any decision you do not approve of in regards to your situation."

"It's true, Olivia. You never let your father or myself coerce you into doing what we think is best. And I hesitate to say this in front of his mother, but I doubt you will let Mr. Jenkins harass you into what he thinks is best either."

Mrs. Jenkins smiled. "I believe this proposal is a perfect example. You won't be pressured into marrying him until you are ready. I applaud that. But I would like to see grandchildren before the Good Lord calls me home."

Olivia said, "Well, despite my apparently normal hesitation, there are other reasons."

Mrs. Jenkins sat back to get comfortable. "And they are?"

Olivia blushed. "Well. . ."

"Let me make this easy for you, Miss Blakesley. Do you love my son?"

"There is nothing not to love."

"That wasn't the question."

Olivia sighed. "I refuse because I love him. I will never be a biddable wife, never take tea, go to operas, or follow the latest fashions. I will do as I have always done. Paint the stars, read my journals, and go my own way. That is nobody's definition of a good wife, Mrs. Jenkins."

"A very pretty defense. But Nathaniel would be bored silly with a biddable wife, will never know the latest fashions either, and abhors the opera. You two seem perfect for each other. And despite all your talk I think that is what you are afraid of. You have met your match, my dear."

Mrs. Blakesley beamed at Mrs. Jenkins. "I thought the same thing. It comforts me to know you agree, Mrs. Jenkins."

Olivia shook her head. "It really is quite a pity then that one of the parties involved has no intention of changing her mind about this marriage business."

Mrs. Jenkins put her cup down. She cleared her throat. She looked to Mrs. Blakesley and said quietly, "Would you mind if I had a moment alone with your daughter, Mrs. Blakesley?"

Mrs. Blakesley looked reproachfully at Olivia, then stood. "Good luck, Mrs. Jenkins."

Mrs. Jenkins studied Olivia until the door latched. She leaned forward.

"I applaud your tenacity. If I didn't think you were being a fool, I would congratulate you on remaining true to your principles. If I hadn't heard with my own ears that you love my son, I would say no woman should be forced to marry. And yet, you are an idiot."

Olivia remained silent.

"Know this, Miss Blakesley. My son finds you a fascinating challenge. I have not seen him so happy or alive in many years, and I would accept nearly any girl who could make him smile as much as you do."

She stood. "I hope you are prepared for a siege, my dear. The Jenkins do not give up so easily."

Eleven

Olivia crept through the darkness, cursing herself for all the foolish ideas she had ever come up with. It seemed that old age was not giving the wisdom promised. Indeed not, since this was by far her maddest scheme yet.

Nathaniel would probably not even be at home and the evening would be wasted.

Where was she to sleep tonight? She couldn't go back home, she'd told her mother she would be staying with Mary. And how would she explain to Mary if she arrived at her house after dark?

She should have left the sneaking to Nathaniel. But that was the problem. He hadn't done any sneaking for days, weeks, months. It felt like an eternity. She counted softly to herself. Two weeks? Was that all? She'd fallen into blithering madness because of two weeks? Nathaniel was right. The act of love was positively addicting.

Olivia peered at the number above the door, praying this was the right one. Dear Lord, what if it wasn't?

She pulled her cloak lower over her face and silently cursed Nathaniel. This was all his fault. He had not come calling since he'd proposed; the last time they'd had any real conversation had been at the Mayes'. Instead, he sent his mother to badger her. Her entire family was pestering her. The one person she wouldn't mind arguing with stayed away.

She missed him.

The man was going to pay.

She knocked discreetly, terror gripping her at the idea that this wasn't his home. What if it was his home but he was not here? Where would she go?

The door was opened by a pair of shiny black boots. "Yes?"

Olivia swallowed and said in a bad French accent, "I am come for Mr. Jenkins. It is a matter of. . . *l'amour.*"

That was greeted with silence and Olivia wanted fervently to hide behind a bush. What had she been thinking!

"I don't suppose you have a card, madam?"

"Um, *non.*"

The shiny black boots sighed. "Please follow me."

He led her down the hall into a study and told her to wait. She looked up after he had gone, studying the comfortable chairs, books stacked on tables, and a fire burning itself out. She sniffed trying to place the scent in the air, wondering if the butler had gone to fetch Nathaniel or the authorities.

The door opened behind her and she quickly looked down again.

"How may I help you, madam?" Nathaniel asked and Olivia nearly swooned with relief.

"Oh, Nathaniel!" She ran to him, throwing herself into his arms.

"Olivia! What's wrong! What has happened!"

She pushed away from him, glaring at him, remembering her anger.

"What's wrong? Where have you been! I've been waiting for you for days, sitting in the damp for nothing!"

He guided her toward the fire, taking off her cloak. He rubbed his forehead.

"Olivia, you refused me. I was staying away to give us both time to think."

"If you'll remember, Mr. Jenkins, we had an agreement. And it had nothing to do with marriage!"

"Sit down, Olivia." He walked to the sideboard, filling a glass and thrusting it at her. "Drink this."

"What is it?" she asked as she sipped, then coughed.

"Brandy. It should warm you up." He stared at her, a perplexed look in his eye. "How did you get here?"

"I hired a hackney from the Rutherford's. I told Mother I was going home with Mary. I walked a distance before choosing one; you know they line up waiting to take everyone home later. I'm amazed it was so easy, really."

Nathaniel slumped into a chair. He muttered to himself, "Is this what marriage would be like? Afraid of the next harebrained scheme my wife would come up with?"

Olivia rose in indignation. "Since we will not be married, that is not in question."

"Then why have you come tonight, if not to accept my hand and tell me how ardently you love and admire me?"

"Don't tease me, Nathaniel. My nerves are shot from all this sneaking around."

"I am not teasing you, Olivia. I am simply wondering why you have gone to the trouble and risk of coming to my home at night?"

She looked at him, unwilling to admit to him that she couldn't go two days without seeing him, two weeks without feeling him. It seemed too pathetic. Better to blame it on curiosity.

He said, "And don't feed me a line of scientific studies. Your parents may buy that mumbo-jumbo but I do not. The stars are the only thing you study."

She sat down. "It's not mumbo-jumbo. I wanted to see you purely for scientific edification."

His eyebrows raised.

"I mean I wanted to see if I could leave undetected and as you are the only one I know I chose to come here. Obviously, it worked quite well."

Nathaniel sat in silence, gazing at her. "So you didn't come to be kissed."

"Of course not. It has only been a few weeks, I assure you I can last that long."

"And you didn't come to investigate my bedroom."

"How shocking!"

He smiled. "I am constantly being surprised by you, my dear. I just wanted to make sure."

"You can be quite sure I have no interest in your *boudoir*, Nathaniel."

"Are you certain? Not even for scientific edification?"

Olivia clasped her hands in her lap. "Well. . . for science. . . I have actually never seen a man's bedroom before."

"That reassures me no end. Shall we?"

He stood, holding his hand out for her.

She took it gingerly, thankful that he had not kicked her out into the night, and thankful he had given her an excuse to stay. Perhaps she could make it up to him. He really was quite patient with her.

He guided her hand through his arm and whispered, "I missed you as well, Olivia."

She pulled her cloak over her head, in case they ran into any servants, and Nathaniel chuckled.

"Do you think that will keep your identity hidden, my dear?"

"It will if you use a little decorum."

"I hate to tell you this but my butler was standing outside the library door listening. I'm quite sure I used your Christian name."

"You should never have got into that bad habit."

"Of course. Would you have preferred me to use your family name, Miss Blak–"

"Nathaniel! Can't you pretend I'm one of your doxies?"

"I am not in the habit of bringing women to my home, Oli–" She glared at him from under her cloak and he corrected himself. "My dear."

Olivia dug into the reticule dangling from her wrist. "I'm sure I shouldn't show you this, since you are behaving quite poorly."

"It's the shock."

"But I thought you might help me with a few scientific inquiries tonight. Since I'm here."

"Indeed?"

She pulled a miniature book out and handed it to him as he opened his bedroom door and ushered her in.

Olivia took a step in, surveying his large four poster bed and dark masculine furnishings. His scent filled the air and she breathed deeply. She had entered the lion's lair. Forbidden territory. It was all quite exciting.

She said, "Your bed is quite a bit bigger than mine."

She turned to find him flipping through her naughty book. He looked up at her. "Olivia, this is a. . . This book is about. . ."

She grinned and hopped onto his bed. "It's quite dirty, isn't it? Page thirty-two, if you please."

Nathaniel cleared his throat and turned to a well done drawing showing a couple in obvious ecstasy. The woman was on all fours, the man bent over behind her, his hands caressing her breasts.

"Where did you get this?"

She waved her hand in the air. "That's not important."

"Yes, it is."

She sighed. "I ordered it through the post, directing it to a Mr. Oliver Balkesley. My family thought it quite diverting and insisted on calling me Oliver Balkesley for months after."

"And no one asked to see it? They weren't curious as to what a mysteriously misdirected package contained?"

"Nathaniel, I am constantly receiving packages in the post. I told them it was a pocket guide to the stars."

Nathaniel folded his arms. "You have entirely too much freedom."

She laughed. "Which is what I've been telling you." She paused and looked at him expectantly.

He cleared his throat again. "I should say no."

"Why?"

"A misguided attempt to curb your impetus?"

She raised an eyebrow. "I believe you are too far gone down this road to become morally superior now, sir." She pointed to the little book clasped in his hands. "Have you ever performed such a feat?"

He groaned. "Olivia."

"I suspect you have, else you would have been outraged at such a suggestion. I would like to experience it please. If you feel up to it, that is."

She couldn't quite keep the smirk off her face after her pun. She finally understood what that meant.

Nathaniel said, "Shall I throw you to the bed and ravish you, then?"

Olivia clapped her hands. "Oh, would you please! You be the dashing pirate and I'll be the innocent virgin you have stolen to satisfy your diabolical lusts."

Nathaniel laughed. "You were never an innocent virgin and the only one with diabolical lusts in this room is you."

"Then you be the innocent virgin and I the dashing, devilish pirate. Hand me your pants, sirrah!"

He groaned. "I have no idea where half your ideas come from."

"That's the trouble with genius, so hard to follow. Now come here and let me ravish you."

He obeyed. "I don't know if it's possible for you to ravish me."

She pulled him closer, grabbing his backside and squeezing. "I think I'll try, nonetheless. Shall I help you with your boots?"

He sat beside her, stroking her hair, and kissed her. Her tongue melded to his, thrusting and parrying.

She knelt before him, pulling on his boots, and said, "I think this position is in that book, too. Perhaps that is how women ravish men."

He groaned. "I fear my heart is not quite ready for such a sight as that."

Ah well, all in good time.

One boot hit the floor with a thud and the second quickly followed.

His breeches melded to his thighs and his arousal pressed firmly against the front. She peeled the breeches off, flinging them to the floor.

He lay on the bed, half-naked, and Olivia carefully inspected every inch of him. For once there was light enough.

"Olivia. You have no idea what you're doing to me, do you?"

"I can imagine. Now off with your shirt."

"Yes, ma'am."

Twelve

Olivia woke next to a warm body, a heavy leg trapping her.

She shoved against it, whispering, "Nathaniel, I can't feel my leg."

He grunted and slid his leg off.

She cuddled beside him, his arm snaking around her.

"Good morning, Olivia."

"Good morning. It's quite nice waking up with you, even if you did crush my leg. You're very warm."

He grinned. "Just think, Olivia, that could be yours every morning if we married."

"Harrumph. Why do you have to ruin a perfectly good morning."

"It's my nature. Would you like breakfast?"

"What about the servants?"

"I'll have them make up a tray." He winked. "That, too, could be yours every morning."

Olivia sniffed. "As if I was so lazy. And I believe my waking up in a man's bed is proof positive that I would not make a good wife."

"As long as it was my bed you woke up in, I believe you would make a very good wife." He began ticking off his fingers. "Because you are entertaining. You are intelligent. You are passionate. You have irresistible taste in dresses. And you make this mewling sound in the back of your throat when you come. I really can find nothing wrong with the idea of marriage."

"I have thought of a new rule, Nathaniel."

He murmured, "Only one?"

"No more mentions of marriage.

It quite puts me off. And stop sending your family to change my mind. I have had enough lectures. I'm surprised you haven't sent for the magistrates. *Tie this girl up, she refuses to marry me.*"

"I could quite easily force your hand, Olivia. You are in my bed, we have had intimate relations. Your father has the right to force me to marry you at sword-point."

"Well, he wouldn't force me at sword-point and I would advise you not to try either."

Nathaniel flung the covers off and rose. He said, "If you do not wish to be forced into marriage, I would advise that you dress quickly. I'll need to deposit you somewhere less questionable."

"You can take me back home. I'll tell them I woke early."

"Lies come unnervingly quick to you, Olivia. Won't your mother ask your sister?"

"No. I go over often enough, she doesn't question it."

He shook his head and muttered, "Too much freedom, entirely."

The cold ring of steel silenced the crickets mid-song. Nathaniel pushed Olivia behind him, cursing himself for escorting her this early in the morning.

Olivia gasped. "Rufus! What are you doing?"

He answered coldly. "I could ask the same of you, Olivia. And of you, Jenkins."

She muttered, "Oh, bother," under her breath and attempted to push Nathaniel aside.

"He has a drawn sabre, Olivia. Please stay behind me."

Her very angry brother-in-law gazed in fury at Nathaniel, and truth be told, he couldn't fault the look. He deserved everything he got from the wicked looking sword. But he'd be damned if he got it in front of Olivia.

Nathaniel said, "Mr. Eliot–"

"Unless you are going to tell me the announcement has already been sent to the papers, I don't want to hear it, Jenkins."

Olivia shouted, "Rufus!"

"Olivia, he is escorting you home in the early morning. And you told your mother you would be staying with us last night."

She gasped again. "You didn't tell her. . ."

". . .No."

"Oh, thank you. I'm sorry, it was a dreadful thing to do, but–"

"It was a stupid thing to do. You are not only risking your reputation but your entire family's as well."

Olivia said, "Yes, well, luckily I'm the only one unmarried."

Nathaniel interrupted. "And luckily, I have already asked for Miss Blakesley's hand."

The sharp end of the sword gently fell to earth. "Good. But this is still a stupid idea, Jenkins."

Olivia tugged at his coat. "Uh, Nathaniel–"

"She however has refused me."

She uttered a very unladylike word as Rufus speared her with his iron-gaze.

"How extraordinary."

"Rufus–"

"If you have no feelings for him, Olivia, why are you sneaking around with him?"

Nathaniel turned to face her, secure in the knowledge that he would not be stabbed in the back by her angry relative. Mr. Eliot's anger was directed where it should rightfully be.

"Yes, Olivia. That question has been bothering me as well."

Her eyes narrowed, her chin rose, and she tapped her foot. "As I have explained, at length, I do not wish to marry."

Rufus Eliot guffawed. "It seems to me that you wish very much to marry."

Olivia blushed. "You know nothing of it, Rufus. And you, Mr. Jenkins, know what this is and why

I won't marry you. Rufus, please escort me home. It would be a disaster if anyone else saw us together."

"It'll give me a chance to tan your backside."

"I dare you to try."

Nathaniel rubbed his forehead. "I'll leave you to it, Eliot. And you, Olivia, I shall see later."

He spun on his heel, frustration flashing in his eyes.

Olivia sighed, cursing herself for her brainless ideas. Cursing the world in general, and men in particular, for making mountains out of mole hills.

Rufus sheathed his sabre, his jaw tight.

"Please don't tell Mary, Rufie."

"Why not? You don't seem to care who knows."

"I care! I was just stupid."

"Olivia, you are walking a tightrope. Jenkins has every right to force you into marriage; he is being too soft-headed. One word to your father would end this."

"Rufus Eliot, you know nothing of the matter. And not you, nor Father, nor Mr. Jenkins, will make me do what I don't want to. So tell the whole world if you want."

Olivia stomped off. She could hear Rufus muttering and following behind her. This plan was going downhill and she wondered if she'd ever been in control of this experiment. Men were a lot harder to understand than the stars.

Mary's strident tones echoed through the house. "Hello, Mother. Where's Olivia?"

Olivia cursed Rufus and then herself. He couldn't keep his big mouth shut and she had been the fool to try and sneak about.

Mary peeked her head around the door and Olivia glared at her. "I am going to kill your toad of a husband."

"Mmm. I believe you have some

explaining to do."

"He could have kept his big mouth shut."

"And you could have stayed at home. Now tell me, was it your idea to sneak off with Mr. Jenkins? Or did he pressure you in some way."

Olivia sighed. "It was my stupid idea. I wanted to see him and I wanted to know if I could sneak away undetected. Obviously I forgot to plan for sneaking back."

"Obviously." Mary sat beside her and stared. "So?"

"So what?"

Mary wiggled her eyebrows. "So how was your first night alone with a man?"

"Mary!"

"Olivia!"

Olivia wiped her brush on the cloth. "It was enjoyable."

"Enjoyable. This was your first night together, wasn't it?"

Olivia refused to look at her. How could she tell Mary that it wasn't?

Mary laughed. "You little sneak. Don't tell me you've snuck off with him before."

Oh, to confide in someone. Mary didn't seem upset with her and it would be nice to share her secrets. She and Mary had always been close.

Olivia glanced at her. "He came here. After dark."

"Ah. So it's not only the stars you've been studying. How is your Mr. Jenkins, then?"

"Mary! Now you want details? You wouldn't give me any after you married Rufus. Technically, this is all your fault. If you had told me anything, anything at all, I wouldn't have needed to conduct such an experiment. I would have taken your word on the subject."

Mary said, "And stowed it away, problem solved. I know you, Olivia. You have never worried about pleasing Mama and finding a husband, and you're too independent to think you need one. What does that leave? You would die a spinster, living your whole life under Papa's roof, having the run of everything, exactly as you please."

"I'm sorry, is something wrong with that scenario? It seems quite pleasant to me."

"Thankfully, I know better. That is boring, Livvy. Yes, yes, you would have your studies, but no family. No interruptions, no surprises. Having a plan is all well and good, but distractions are sometimes better."

Olivia raised her eyebrows. "I find this hard to believe coming from someone who has known who she would marry since she was five years old."

"That wasn't a plan, Livvy, that just was. I can't help it if I found my mate so young."

"So you want me to have distractions. That's why you wouldn't tell me about your wedding night." Olivia narrowed her eyes. "It was your wedding night, wasn't it?"

Mary gave her a small smile. "Of course it was my wedding night, as we were married that day. But was that the first time we were intimate? That was the night before we became engaged. Rufus was so distraught about the whole thing he ran to Father the next day."

"I can't believe you never told me!"

"I didn't tell you because I didn't want you getting any ideas. That was clearly short-sighted of me; you don't need my help in thinking up crazy ideas."

Olivia balled her fist and pounded her leg. "And I can't believe your toady husband was so self-righteously smug!"

"Olivia, you have a strange concept of the world. Rufus, although of course he loved me, had ruined me, therefore he had to marry me. Mr. Jenkins has ruined you, therefore he has to marry you."

"Our situations are vastly different, Mary. You were but eighteen and I am twenty-seven. If you and Rufus and Nathaniel will simply be quiet about it, no one need know that I am ruined. It's not as if I was marriageable material before, anyway."

Mary fingered the paint pots. "Do you not like Mr. Jenkins?"

"Well, of course I like him. I would not have done such a thing if I didn't."

Mary eyed her. "Sometimes I think it doesn't matter if you like the idea or not, as long as you find a solution to your problem."

Olivia glared at her. "That is a terrible thing to say. I am not immoral."

"I believe the vicar would argue that."

"I believe the vicar would argue that you are immoral. Simply because you married afterward does not change the fact."

Mary shrugged. "The vicar would likely argue that the king is immoral."

"The king *is* immoral."

"So he is. But that doesn't change the fact that you are a ruined woman. You must marry Mr. Jenkins. Soon, Olivia. There are consequences to your actions that will not wait for you to change your mind."

Olivia stared out the window. "There is nothing to worry on that regard, Mary. There are no unexpected consequences."

"Do you not wish to have children?"

Olivia glanced at her. A touchy subject, she knew. "I am an aunt many times over. That's enough for me."

Mary snorted. "You can lie to yourself, Livvy, but I at least know there is a vast difference between being an aunt and a mother."

"I know, but it doesn't call to me.

I don't lie awake picturing my child."

Mary rubbed her belly lightly, then nodded. "I understand. It won't be the end of the world if you don't have one."

"No matter what Mama thinks. How many grandchildren does one woman need?"

"I think she wants granddaughters."

Olivia conceded the point. The newest generation *was* overrun with boys.

Mary said, "What of Mr. Jenkins?"

"What of him?"

"Where does he stand in all this? I thought you liked him. I thought he liked you."

"I do like him, and I believe he does like me. But that was never part of our agreement. He agreed to certain rules."

Olivia sighed. She should end it now. She should write him a quick note telling him his services were no longer needed. She didn't know if she could do it, though. How could she give up the best times of her life? Why should she have to?

Damn men and their rules. Damn marriage. She could be quite happy as a kept woman. As long as she was Nathaniel's kept woman. What need had she of society? She could endure the jeers of the *ton*, the insults. Oh, if only she was an only child, with no family to suffer for her actions.

Mary looked intrigued at the idea of an agreement but merely said, "Agreements change, Olivia. You like him, he likes you. Why are we having this conversation? We should be celebrating your engagement."

"It is marriage I do not care for."

"What have you against marriage?"

"Have you met our parents? They're miserable."

Mary studied her. "I don't think they're miserable."

"They have nothing in common, rarely talk to each other, and remember the fights they used to have? I'm surprised any of us married."

"I don't remember them fighting. And they have six children in common. I think that's something."

Olivia sighed. "You've been in love with Rufus since before you could walk. You were oblivious to our parents strife."

"And you are too sensitive. You notice every little detail, but miss the big picture. They're happy together now, don't you agree?"

Olivia shrugged. "They seem resigned."

Mary narrowed her eyes. "What of Rufus and me? Do you think that we fight all the time and have nothing to talk about and nothing in common?"

"No."

"But?"

Olivia pinched her lips. "But I don't think it will last. I don't want to be mean, but I've never seen any marriage stay happy. For instance, Prudence. She's so miserable, I can hardly stand to be around her."

"Prudence is pregnant with her fifth child in six years and you know how swollen she gets at the end. I don't think that's a fair example. Besides, just the fact that this is the fifth baby means that she and Marcus have something in common."

"A bed."

Mary laughed. "Yes, a bed. And don't knock it. Prue could keep him out if she wanted. Just as Mama could have kept Papa out and they had six."

Olivia shook her head. "I know she has what she wants, as does Mama, and so do you. It's just. . . It's just that I don't want it. I don't want to be stuck with someone that I hate, eating meals in silence, or relying on my children for love. I don't want that, Mary."

"And you think that will happen

with Mr. Jenkins?"

"It's inevitable. One day he will look at me with loathing instead of passion. One day he will think himself a fool for letting his emotions push him into marrying so unsuitably. I need only look at Papa to see how it will happen." She shook her head and whispered, "I could not bear it if I saw Nathaniel look at me like that."

Mary took her hand gently. "I never realized how pessimistic you are."

"I'm realistic. I refuse to be blinded by love."

"No, you're blinded by fear."

Olivia was silent.

Mary patted her arm. "You are not Mama, Mr. Jenkins is not Papa. If anyone can have a marriage worthy of love, it is you, Livvy. You can make anything work. The only question is, do you want to make it work with Mr. Jenkins?"

Thirteen

"Aunt Livvy, Aunt Livvy! We have a surprise for you!"

"You do?" Olivia grunted as she caught her five-year-old nephew as he flung himself into her arms.

Olivia's eldest sister Prudence lumbered from the coach. "Yes, but not yet, Richie. It's a surprise."

"I told her it was a surprise."

"Hmm. We'll have to work on that."

Olivia let Richie go as he spied his cousins. She kissed Prue on the cheek and said, "How's the little devil?"

Prue grunted. "This is the last

one, I swear. I can't sleep, I can't eat, and my ankles! I look like a cow."

"You've said each one was the last one, so I can hardly believe you now."

"I keep having boys! Four boys in a row! Even God could not be so cruel. I deserve a girl, surely."

Olivia said, "And if this one's a boy?"

"Don't curse me. If this one's a boy, Marcus will be sleeping with his horses."

"Mmm. And you'll have another. Mother didn't learn her lesson until she had six. I doubt you'll give up before then either."

Prudence groaned. "Every night I pray to God that I will do anything, *anything,* if He'll just make sure this one is a girl."

"Then how can He refuse. Come, Prue. I have a seat all set up for you in the pasture."

Prudence swatted her. "Just wait until you start waddling around. I'll not hold my glee." Prudence eyed her. "Is your Mr. Jenkins coming today?"

"He is not my Mr. Jenkins."

"I think the lady doth protest too much. He is certainly no one else's. He only dances with you at balls, I hear. Two dances, then poof."

Olivia narrowed her eyes. "I'm going to cut out Mary's tongue."

"Tut-tut. Does your Mr. Jenkins know how violent you are? Oh, never fear, dear. I certainly won't tell him. He'll find out soon enough after the wedding when you lock him in his bedroom so you can paint in peace."

Was Olivia never to live that down? She had been in braids when she had pulled that little stunt.

She changed the subject. "Have you heard if Eugenia is coming today?"

"She said she would try, although she is feeling a little under the weather." Prudence winked. "I believe a wedding-night baby is on the way."

"Egad. Two sisters expecting at the same time? How will we ever survive."

"Mmm. At least I'm almost done. I feel bad for Mary, though. She laughed it off when Amelia became pregnant right away, but it has been four years now. What will she think when she hears about Eugenia?"

Olivia said, "Probably the same thing I thought when I heard Eugenia was getting married. Rot her. The youngest should never do anything before the eldest have had their turn."

Prudence chuckled. "I would have given you my monthly allowance if you'd said that to Eugenia when she was getting married. Perhaps I'll mention it to Mary."

Luncheon was served picnic-style. Cold ham, diced potatoes, and light wine. The men and children sprawled in the grass; the ladies sat in chairs.

Eugenia stood up and announced that, yes, she was in the family way.

Mrs. Blakesley clapped her hands, the men congratulated Landon, and Mr. Blakesley said, "We can never have too many babies."

Olivia snorted. If this family had anything in excess, it was babies.

Mary entered the melée with, "Rot you, Eugenia," and everyone turned to stare at her.

Prudence hid her chortle behind a very loud cough that turned into a real fit. Olivia pounded her on the back.

Eugenia fingered her lace collar. "I'm sorry, Mary. I don't mean to be cruel but just because you can't have a baby doesn't mean everyone can't be happy for me."

Mary looked unperturbed. "I can have a baby, you twit. I simply wanted to tell everyone first."

Prudence stopped coughing. "Are

you truly?"

Mary patted her tummy. "Around Christmas."

Mrs. Blakesley jumped from her chair and ran to hug Mary. "A Christmas baby!"

Marcus leaned toward Rufus and whispered, "About bloody time. Prudence wanted me to see if you needed any tips," and Rufus turned bright red.

Prudence narrowed her eyes. "I don't remember you being ill at all."

Mary smirked. "Not a stitch. Felt better than ever."

"Rot you."

Mrs. Blakesley frowned at her. "Prudence, language!"

Olivia rubbed her forehead. "Three sisters? That's half the Blakesley bunch. I hope one of you has a girl. Poor little Margaret is surrounded over there by seven boys."

Eugenia stamped her foot. "Hello! I'm pregnant as well,

Mama!"

Mrs. Blakesley hugged her. "I know, dear. And we are excited about that as well. It's just we've been waiting so long for Mary."

"I don't see why that makes any difference."

Prudence sighed. "That's because you've never learned the art of anticipation, Eugenia. The longer it takes, the better it is. That's why Olivia's wedding is going to be the best of the bunch. Because we've all been waiting so long."

Mrs. Blakesley speared her third oldest daughter with *the look*, but it was too late.

"Rot you, Prue."

Eugenia sat beside Olivia. "Is your Mr. Jenkins coming today? I should think we'd all like to meet him."

Mary hid a snigger behind her hand and Olivia glared at her.

"No. And he's not my Mr. Jenkins."

"Really? The way Mary tells it,

the engagement is as good as announced."

"Mary is a twit."

Mrs. Blakesley clapped her hands. "That is enough, girls! There are children present."

Little Richie peeked out from behind his father's chair and said, "Twit."

Prudence leaned over and whispered, "Don't worry, Livvy. He didn't learn that from you." She pointed a finger at her eavesdropping child. "Run off and play with your cousins, Richie."

"But when are we going to give Aunt Livvy her surprise?"

Mr. Blakesley jumped up. "Quite right. Shall we go get it, Richie?"

"Yes!"

Olivia turned to Mary. "And have you all known about this surprise?"

Eugenia grinned. "Of course we have. And I'm surprised Mary didn't let you in on it."

Olivia was surprised, too. Mary shrugged. "I would have told you if

I'd thought you wouldn't like it."

"That is comforting."

Mrs. Blakesley swatted at Mary. "Oh, it's quite exciting. I think, Olivia, that you will be over the moon."

Richie ran across the lawn, waving a small wrapped package, Grandpapa trailing behind him.

Olivia said, "I'll have to assume it's not breakable."

Margaret and six more little boys came running over to sit by Aunt Livvy.

Richie held the gift in his hands. "You must wait for Grandpapa."

Olivia nodded. "May I hold it?"

Prue shook her head. "Don't give it to her until Grandpapa is here. We don't want her cheating."

"Mama says no, Aunt Livvy."

"Well then, what does it feel like?"

A chorus of yells and boos greeted her question and she sat back, grinning at her family. It wasn't even her birthday. A thought crossed her mind that it had something to do with Nathaniel and she nearly groaned. What would her family do when she broke off their agreement and never saw him again? Hang her, most likely.

Mr. Blakesley resumed his chair. "Go ahead, Richie. Let her open it."

Richie solemnly handed her the gift and Olivia felt through the wrapping. She bent it in half, and looked up.

"It feels like a magazine."

The children yelled at her to open it, and so she did. She looked for a moment in consternation.

"It's my monthly star magazine. Have you renewed my subscription?"

Mrs. Blakesley leaned forward. "No, silly. Open it."

She opened it and read the contents page and felt the blood drain from her face.

"My article," she whispered. "They published my article."

Mr. Blakesley leaned forward. "With drawings! Look at the article, my dear. Everything is in detail. Quite extraordinary. None of the other articles have drawings half so well done."

"You sent in my article to be published after they'd already rejected it?"

"And look, Olivia," Mrs. Blakesley leaned forward," with your own name, not some silly fake one."

She looked up at her family, all smiling and happy for her, and bit back her retort. Not some silly fake name? This was exciting? The entire world was going to laugh at her. Oh, her family thought it fun that she studied the stars, but it wasn't going to impress anybody else. It would just make them laugh harder.

She said numbly, "Thank you."

Prudence nudged her. "Come, Olivia. Is that all you have to say? Your name! In a respected journal."

Olivia looked down again, scanning her article, eying her drawings. She had hoped one day to find her work accepted. But the article had needed more work. And she definitely wouldn't have used her own name!

"It's overwhelming. I can't think what to say."

Her father smiled. "Let the poor girl get her head around it. It's not every day the Blakesley name is put in print."

Marcus slapped his knee. "Well, pass it around. Let us have a look at it."

The children gathered around him and they loudly exclaimed at the drawings.

Mr. Blakesley winked at her. "Well done, Livvy."

Olivia smiled, wondering how big a debacle this would create.

Mary slipped her arm through Olivia's and steered her towards the trees. "You hated it. Even I thought you would be excited."

"You thought I would like having my name bandied about?

"Oh, Olivia. No one will care a fig if you've published in a magazine. I doubt anyone will even know."

"Did none of you think this would cause a stir in society?"

"Olivia, no one but you reads those dreadfully dull tomes. And no, I don't think it will cause a stir. Why should it?"

"Because I am already odd man out, that's why."

Mary eyed her. "Are you worried about your Mr. Jenkins reaction?"

"Aaargh! He is not my Mr. Jenkins."

Mary laughed. "Of course not. Anyway, everyone in the family is quite proud of you. Especially Papa. And I know you don't care at all what society thinks of you anyway. We shall simply see if Mr. Jenkins is worthy of you, shan't we?"

Fourteen

Olivia heard the murmurings as soon as she entered the ballroom. She hissed at Mary, "See. No one will care a fig, my ars–"

"Miss Blakesley, tell me is it true? Do you write for a magazine?" Miss Emily Mayes fluttered her fan. Oh, to confirm this scandal would be the height of the season.

Olivia took a deep breath. "I fear I don't know what you are referring to."

Miss Mayes slipped her arm through Olivia's and walked her round the ring of on-lookers. "Well, according to Papa, there was an entry in this month's star journal done by a Miss Olivia Blakesley."

"Hmm. I would like to see that. But Miss Mayes, it's not an uncommon name. Perhaps there is another Olivia Blakesley."

"Who is batty over the stars?"

"That is a bit of a coincidence, but I assure you, I would never send an article to a magazine." Under her own name.

Olivia bit back her anger. How dare her family do this to her. Was it not enough to be the black sheep of the family, did they have to advertise that fact?

Mary came to rescue her, expertly slipping between Miss Mayes and Olivia.

"Miss Mayes. Have you heard the news?"

"Indeed I have. Although Miss Blakesley is playing dumb."

Mary looked confused for a moment, then waved her hand. "Oh, that. Diverting isn't it, that there could be two Olivia

Blakesley's nutty over the stars? But have you heard about Caroline Drew? She has gone to the continent!"

Miss Mayes sucked in her breath. "No!"

Olivia slunk away, thankful for Mary and her gossip for once in her life. Poor Miss Drew's exodus to the continent during the season could only mean one thing in the eyes of the *ton*. Poor Miss Drew had been ruined and she was leaving to hide the evidence. For one brief moment Olivia felt a little sympathy nausea for Poor Miss Drew. What if Olivia needed to escape to the continent?

Dear Lord.

"Hello, my dear," a soft voice murmured behind her.

She turned unsteadily. "Mr. Jenkins."

One eyebrow arched at her, funning her attempt at formality. "I thought we were passed all that, Olivia."

She shook her head. "I have

begun to rethink my actions in light of this latest news."

"Come, Olivia. You don't think an article in a scientific journal would make me think less of you?"

For an instant her anger resurfaced. "My damn family."

Nathaniel chuckled. "Indeed, it must be slightly embarrassing for you, but you seem to be handling it. And, in all truth, the article doesn't surprise me at all. I think you are capable of anything."

"I don't think that was a compliment, Nathaniel."

He squeezed her hand. "You should take it as such."

"But that wasn't what I was rethinking. Poor Miss Drew has made me reconsider our agreement."

"Aah."

"Yes, aah. What if–"

"My dear, Miss Drew's situation and your own have nothing in common. If the unthinkable happened, then I would simply kidnap you and tie you to a horse until we had reached Scotland."

Olivia's mouth dropped open and she stared at him. Why, he seemed quite cheerful about the prospect.

"Mr. Jenkins! You would do no such thing!"

"I would. I've been considering it already."

Olivia had nothing to say to that.

Nathaniel said, "Shall we dance, my dear?"

"I don't think that's a good idea."

"Oh? Do you think attracting everyone's attention back to yourself after being so fortuitously diverted by Miss Drew is a better one? I shudder to think what rumors would circulate if we did not dance together. A falling out, perhaps? Or do I disapprove of my future wife having her name published? I can think of no better way to acknowledge your accomplishment, my dear."

Olivia narrowed her eyes. "You have a serious flaw, Mr. Jenkins."

He bowed, his eyes twinkling. He swept her on to the dance floor, holding her at a respectable distance.

He said, "Your brother-in-law is glaring daggers at me."

She sighed. "I will have a word with him. I am sorry, Nathaniel."

"I don't think speaking with him will alleviate the situation, Olivia. I have taken advantage of you, I must make repairs. Or perhaps you would tell him that you took advantage of me? He might not believe you, but it is a generous offer."

"You are being uncommonly cruel tonight."

"I apologize. I am uncommonly frustrated. I was told you were stubborn, but I had not expected to find a mule in so becoming a bonnet."

Olivia gritted her teeth. "And I had not expected to find a jackass in hat and tails."

He quickly covered his guffaw

with a large cough, smiling his apologies at the other couples.

He held her tighter for one moment, before letting her move to a more polite distance.

He said softly, "Marry me."

"Why?"

"Because I have never found another lady who could call me vulgar names while waltzing. It's intoxicating."

"You are very strange, Nathaniel."

"We are a perfect match then, aren't we?"

Olivia bit back her answer. For one moment, she had almost agreed with him. "Nathaniel–"

"If you're going to berate me, I'll have you know it will do no good. I am just as stubborn as you."

"More so, I would say. I was merely going to remind you of the No Marriage Rule. You agreed to not bring it up."

He shook his head. "I don't believe I did, my dear."

"Yes, you did. When we began our tra–"

"If you call our relationship a transaction, I shall dump you on the floor."

"–relationship, you agreed to abide by my rules."

"I don't believe I did. I agreed to listen to your rules and tell you if they're complete twaddle. This No Marriage Rule is complete twaddle and I won't abide by it."

Olivia stared at him in frustration. "If we weren't dancing I would bash you over the head with my reticule."

"Then it's a good thing we're dancing. Are you free for the next one as well, my dear?"

A small growl escaped her throat and Nathaniel grinned down at her. "If I had any compassion at all, I would leave you alone. Alas."

"You are deliberately goading me."

"Yes. It livens things up a bit for me. And it confuses your brother-in-law. He doesn't know who to glare at, you or me."

Olivia had thought women were the diabolical schemers, the ones unable to think of anything but marriage. Nathaniel and Rufus would give the most intense mama a run for her money.

Nathaniel twirled them around the dance floor, keeping hold of her between dances, ignoring her token protest. At this point, no one would be surprised at two dances in a row.

He said, "I trust, my dear, you have no adventures planned for this evening?"

She scowled. "You trust correctly. While it was quite exhilarating, I found the ending not to my liking. I have no desire to run into Rufus again; no doubt he would be dragging a vicar along with him this time."

She looked at him from the corner of her eye. "Do you have any adventures planned for this evening?"

"Perhaps. If I can find the fortitude to brave the cold, the hard, the unrelenting."

Olivia shook her head, her eyes beseeching the heavens. "Fortitude may not be necessary; I am not out there studying the stars every night. Perhaps you will discover there is no one to share the cold and the hard with you."

"A fate I would no doubt deserve."

She said, "Indeed," and he laughed.

Nathaniel escorted her back to Mary. Olivia glared daggers at her sister. She would not put it past Mary to demand Nathaniel's declaration here and now. And Olivia feared he would oblige, professing his undying love for everyone to hear.

Thankfully, they remembered propriety, though Mary conversed with an evil twinkle in her eye. The headache that had weakened in

Nathaniel's company came back with force, and Olivia excused herself as soon as he left.

She found a quiet chair, hidden slightly by a tall potted plant, and allowed herself a moment to relax. She wondered briefly if she had the stamina to continue fighting Nathaniel and her family. She was finding them more wearisome than she'd expected.

Conversation flowed around her, easily ignored, until she heard a strident feminine voice say, "And there goes Mr. Jenkins. He's done his two with Miss Blakesley."

A second woman snickered. "And still no announcement. What is the delay, I wonder?"

"Someone must have an objection to the match, his mother perhaps? Her family must be over the moon. If I was Miss Blakesley, I would be pressing for an announcement soon. An angry mother-in-law would be worth the prize. She can't afford to lose him at this point;

who knows how she managed to snare him."

The women wandered off and Olivia remained sitting behind her plant. She was not surprised by their conversation. She only felt sorrow that Nathaniel and his family suffered from such gossip.

She sighed, a heartfelt sound that seemed to encapsulate her predicament perfectly, and then rose tiredly to find her family. She could not bear to stay any longer.

Despite her threats, Nathaniel found Olivia exactly where he thought she would be. It was a clear night, after all.

She was sitting in her chair, her sketchbook lying at her feet. She glanced in his direction, then returned to her stars. He sat companionably at her feet, watching with her. A few clouds skidded across the night sky.

"Tell me why your father allows

you outside any night you wish."

"He really didn't have any say in the matter. When he found I'd been sneaking out, he grounded me and took away my telescope. So I stole the house keys and locked everyone in their bedrooms while I went outside to paint."

"Remind me not to forbid you anything you desire."

He looked down at her sketchbook. "May I?"

Olivia nodded, trying to see her art with new eyes. Trying to see what the world saw. A hopeless hack? Or a passionate artist?

He flipped the papers, then looked back up at her. "Tell me why you study the stars so."

Olivia pointed to a group of stars, sketching the shape with her finger. "That's the great bear, Ursa Major. It always comes back to the same place in the night sky, but it's always moving. Predictable, but not stagnant."

Nathaniel watched her. "Olivia, I

didn't tell you the most important reason why I wanted to marry you." She looked down at him. "I love you. Now that I have found you, I cannot live without you."

She looked so sad, her faced bathed in moonlight. "I could never marry anyone other than you, Nathaniel, but I'm afraid."

"I didn't think you were afraid of anything. You sit outside alone at night and proposition strange men."

She smiled slightly. "You were never strange. I knew you at first glance."

"So what are you afraid of? You know me." He pointed at the stars and grinned. "I'm always the same and predictable, but never stagnant."

He rose to his knees, kissing her gently. "I love you, Olivia. Be my bright light in the darkness."

She grabbed his hand, willing herself not to cry. "Nathaniel. You have been so patient, waiting for me to realize how much you love me, how much I love you. And I do."

He kissed her, his eyes shining.

"But I will not change my mind. No matter the advice my family heaps on me, no matter how kind-hearted you are, no matter the promises you make. Marriage and I do not mix. I can't marry you. And it has been cruel of me to keep you. Your sister told me that you deserved a family. Wife and children and a happy home. You do. More than anyone I have ever known, you deserve to be happy."

Nathaniel stared at her, his face closed. "So you wish to continue with this, then? Sneaking about, hard grounds, whispers behind fans. You enjoy this?"

Olivia stood, clutching her sketch pad to her chest. "No. You have taught me passion, and lust, and love. Everything I wanted to learn. It was never meant to go on forever. I believe our transaction is over."

He flinched, his jaw clenched, and he looked past her shoulder.

Olivia willed the tears not to fall. She could not marry him, and she could not go on as they were. The humane thing was to let him go, let him live his life without her.

She said, "I hope you find a–"

"If that is your last word on the matter, I will leave you to your stars. Goodbye, Miss Blakesley."

He strode from her angrily, his hands fisted. His eyes met hers as he descended down the ladder and she saw what she had always feared. Hate. Loathing. And hurt.

She whispered, "Goodbye, Nathaniel. I hope you find someone better than me."

Fifteen

Olivia watched sadly as the last of London flew by. Her last season, her last trip to London, the last of balls and rumors and dirty air. She would not be coming back, and for a moment she grew wistful. This year had been different. Nathaniel had changed everything. For once she had not been the object of pitiful stares and fearful comparisons. For once she had not been laughed at. She, Olivia Blakesley, spinster extraordinaire, had been normal.

Except for the article. That hadn't been normal. But Nathaniel's obvious unconcern had shortened the life of the scandal considerably.

Olivia's reputation would be even more infamous now. In the eyes of the *ton* she had either lost or rejected Nathaniel's suit. She would take odds that no one thought she had rejected him. What sane woman would? What sane spinster would?

She sighed, dropping the curtain, and settled back into her seat. Thankfully, she need never hear the whispers, the rumors, again. She would go back to her quiet house and her quiet stars and paint. She would live her life as she planned it, with no distractions, no surprises.

With no Nathaniel.

She had done the right thing. No matter how it hurt to let him go, he deserved better. In a few months, after they had spent time apart, they both would realize their affection for each other had been passing.

She would remember for the rest of her days what it had been like to love and be loved. That was all she had asked for. A moment. Not a lifetime.

That was enough for her. And she would continue to tell herself so until she believed it.

Her father cleared his throat quietly. He had sat across from her in the small confines of the coach reading quietly until now. "I hear Mr. Jenkins asked for your hand. And you refused."

Olivia glanced at him. "Yes. I wasn't sure you knew; you didn't say anything."

"I knew. Your mother has been quite distraught."

She smiled slightly. "Yes, I've heard her. All of London heard her. But Papa, it will work out fine. I've planned it all, and no one should worry. The spinster's life will work well for me. I'll have plenty of time for my studies. And I can run the estate just as well as you can. Marcus will let me stay here after you and Mama have gone."

She touched his arm, apologizing for bringing up a sad subject.

He said, "I do not doubt that you will run the place better than I. But that is not what I'm concerned about."

He looked out the window. "The greatest pleasures I have had in my life have been at home. With my wife and children surrounding me." He sighed. "When you children were young, the house was filled with noise and activity. Scraped knees to be kissed, tears to be dried, dolls to be admired. Looking back at my life, I realize those are the memories I return to time and again. I would not want you to miss that, Olivia. You, of all my children, study and watch and listen. You have great insight into the human condition."

"I like to make sense of life,

Papa."

He smiled and patted her hand. "Yes. But I fear you sometimes prefer to watch rather than do. A student of the wind and waves would not hesitate to jump on a boat or frolic in the ocean to study more deeply. I would not want you to miss this opportunity to study life more in depth. A husband and children would not take from the experience, but add."

Olivia stared unseeing out the window. "But what if I'm afraid?"

"Do you fear Mr. Jenkins?"

"I fear myself. I wonder if I'll forget who I am and try to be his perfect wife."

Mr. Blakesley laughed. "You have never tried to be a perfect anything, Olivia. Not a perfect daughter, a perfect sister, a perfect aunt. You have always walked your own path. I doubt you would stop now. And I doubt Mr. Jenkins would want that since you are the woman he wishes to marry."

"He would probably be quite shocked if I turned up in a frilly orange ball gown."

"The man would probably demand the return of the real Olivia."

"What if he doesn't let me out at night to watch the stars?"

Mr. Blakesley's eyes twinkled.

"Then I dare say you would do the same thing when I forbade you to go outside after dark: Steal all the keys to the bedchambers, lock everyone inside, and continue your studies in peace."

Olivia smiled. "I don't know why you didn't tan my hide."

Mr. Blakesley chuckled. "It wouldn't have done any good."

She looked at her father and said quietly, "How do I know it will be a happily-ever-after?"

"You just have to believe. And be prepared to take some action to get it."

The carriage ride was long and uncomfortable, but at last they arrived. Four boys ran out to greet them, yipping and hollering. Marcus helped her down from the carriage, her backside protesting profusely with every step.

"Ah, Olivia. Have you come to see my wife's pride and joy?"

She smiled. "You know I have. They heard the cry in Scotland, I'm sure. A girl, a girl! Prudence has had her girl!"

Marcus laughed. "If you want anything from her, now is the time to ask. She has already told the boys they may have whatever they wish as a gift from their sister."

"No more threats of Papa sleeping with his horses?"

"I believe I'm safe. For now."

Olivia spied her mother behind him. She had arrived weeks earlier to help Prudence with her lying-in, and Olivia was not looking forward to hearing her mother's thoughts on losing Mr. Jenkins.

But her mother merely looked at her, not saying a word, and went straight to her father, fussing over him and exclaiming how happy she was he had made it safely.

Olivia sighed in relief and instructed one of the boys to take her to Prudence.

She lay on the bed, her daughter asleep in the cradle of her arms. Prudence radiated joy, her eyes bright and shiny.

"Congratulations, Prue."

"Isn't she beautiful, Livvy? The most beautiful sight in the whole world."

Olivia smiled and stroked the baby soft skin of her niece. "Far be it for me to contradict a deliriously happy mama."

"Tell me she is beautiful, Olivia, or I shan't let you hold her."

"She is the most precious thing I have ever seen."

Prudence grinned, relaxing her hold as Olivia took the baby.

Olivia looked down at her niece.

"Have you thought of a name?"

"Nothing. I wouldn't think of it while I was pregnant and now I can't think of a single one. I've been calling her my little angel and the boys have taken it up." Prudence looked at her sheepishly. "What do you think?"

"I think she will be the terror of the house if you name her that. She will boss her brothers around, get whatever she wants from her papa, and be doted upon by her mama."

Prue sighed happily. "I know. She'll be the most spoiled little girl in the whole world."

Olivia grinned down at her niece. "It doesn't sound too bad a life, does it, Angel?"

"Mother is going to have a fit. I can hear her already, *What kind of name is that?*"

"I think I'd surprise her with it at the christening."

They sat companionably, simply admiring the baby. Olivia stroked the wisps of her hair and marveled at the size of her fingernails.

Olivia said, "Mother's not speaking to me."

Prudence rolled her eyes. "Lucky you. I hear all day long about Mr. Jenkins and your rejection of him. Pray that she continues *punishing* you."

Olivia snickered. "How long do you think it will last? Do I have until tomorrow, at least?"

Prudence shook her head. "If she makes it to dinner, I'll eat a goat."

They laughed until a tear slid down Olivia's cheek.

She whispered, "I want this, Prue. I thought I had everything I wanted, but now. . . I feel empty. I feel like a great hole is missing in my life, in my heart."

"Get him back."

She shook her head. "Impossible. You don't know what I did, what I said."

"No, nor do I want to since it was likely unforgivable. You really need to learn to hold your temper."

"Oh, that's rich coming from you."

"What I've found useful is to say I'm sorry. Grovel a bit." Prudence laughed. "Kissing usually loosens up an angry man."

Olivia said, "How have you stayed married for so long? Why hasn't he killed you yet?"

Prudence shrugged, unconcerned. "He loves me, and I him. It's really not so hard, Livvy. May I have my baby back so you can go win over your man?"

Olivia kissed the top of Angel's head and handed her back to Prue.

"Don't think so much, Olivia. Just go."

Sixteen

Olivia arrived back in London after another long carriage ride, dropping her trunk off at Mary's and seizing Rufus' curricle with hardly a hello. She raced to Nathaniel's, arriving breathless and minus her hat. She vaulted from the coach and rang the bell repeatedly. The butler, in his shiny black boots, answered the door with a curt, "Madam!"

"Could you please tell Mr. Jenkins that Miss Olivia Blakesley is here to see him. It is something of an emergency."

"He is not at home, Miss."

"Is he really not or did he just tell you to say that? I know he is mad at me, but I really must talk to him. I need to tell him what a toad I am."

The butler stared at her expressionless. He looked behind him, then leaned toward her conspiratorially. "He has gone to the green."

"Oh, thank you! I could kiss you!"

He reared back in alarm.

"But I won't, of course not. Good day!"

She hopped back into the buggy, crying for the horses to GO!

The cook peeked out from behind the butler and nudged him. "You should have told her he was with that Miss Mayes. That'll be a shocker."

"I have no doubt Miss Blakesley can take Miss Mayes with one hand tied behind her back."

"Ooh, would you like to make a

little wager on that, sir?"

He looked at her in surprise. "Are you betting on Miss Mayes?"

"Course not. Just how long it'll take Miss Blakesley to get rid of her."

"Mmm."

"Nathaniel!"

He turned in surprise to hear his name shouted across the green and stared in disbelief as Olivia came racing through on a curricle.

Miss Mayes peered toward the contraption. "Who is– Is that Miss Blakesley? What is she doing?"

Nathaniel shut his mouth quickly and tugged on his waist coat. "It appears she is trying to run over the pedestrians."

Miss Mayes slipped her hand through Nathaniel's elbow and chuckled. "It does appear that way. Ho, Miss Blakesley, where's the fire?"

Olivia jumped from the rig,

pausing when she saw Miss Mayes. "Are you still wearing that dreadful feather in your hair? Really, Nathaniel, could you not have picked a girl who at least didn't walk around looking like a chicken?"

Miss Mayes screeched, "This is the highest fashion, I'll have you know! And at least he picked someone who knew what fashion was!"

"He doesn't even know what fashion is! He doesn't care! Nor does he like opera, nor does he like balls and dancing. He did all that for me. And he definitely doesn't like silly little girls who think life is about parties and dresses!"

"Oh, you think he would rather have someone who cared for naught but the stars? Who publishes in magazines? Mr. Jenkins is a gentleman, he would never want so low a wife."

Nathaniel watched in amazement as they nearly came to blows. He held Miss Mayes firmly away from Olivia.

"Olivia! What has come over you?"

"You! Look what you've done to me! I was quiet before I met you. Content. Now I'm screaming like a fish wife at Miss Mayes, who I may not have been bosom buddies with but I never hated her. Nathaniel, what are you doing with her?"

"I'm attempting to live my life, Olivia."

Her face crumpled. "But you love me. I am your life. And I was stupid and threw that away, like it was nothing. Like it wasn't the most romantic and sweetest thing anyone has ever said to me. Like you didn't mean it, when I knew you did. When I knew you were the best man I had ever met. The only man I could ever love."

She searched frantically for her handkerchief. Nathaniel handed her his and she buried her face in it. She wailed something into it.

Nathaniel watched her, his heart warming at the ridiculous sight of Olivia flustered and sobbing. "Olivia–"

"I'm a toad!" she cried. "I don't deserve you. But I want you! I want to marry you, and live with you, and wake up with your leg crushing mine–"

Miss Mayes gasped.

"–and argue over who gets to read the paper first, and lock you in the bedroom so I can paint outside, and have little screaming babies who look exactly like you– except not the girls, I would prefer they take after me. Please, Nathaniel. I will be your perfect wife, please."

"I rather think you will be."

Both women looked at him and said, "What?"

"I think you will be the most perfect wife for me, Olivia."

Miss Mayes looked between the two of them– Olivia in her ugly brown dress with buttons to her neck, her hair skewed, hat missing;

Nathaniel, who watched her with obvious admiration.

"I think you both belong in Bedlam."

Nathaniel drew her hand from his arm. "I apologize, Miss Mayes."

She looked between them again. "No, I think this is probably for the best."

She called to her maid, who had stayed well back from the commotion, and walked off– happy to have some very titillating gossip to share.

Olivia stepped closer, gazing into his eyes. "Do you really still want to marry me?"

"God help me, I do."

She frowned. "Did you kiss her?"

"Of course not. She is a proper young lady."

Olivia smiled slowly– hope crowding out the panic, happiness warming the cold.

"I am not a proper young lady."

Nathaniel offered his arm. "Believe me, Olivia, I had noticed.

Would you like to swing by the gazebo before we depart?"

She laughed and entwined her arm with his. "Indeed I would."

Epilogue

Nathaniel climbed the curved wooden staircase, cooing at his crying daughter.

"We'll find your mummy, little one. I'll lay odds ten to one she's up here painting her stars."

He opened the door, the baby giving him away. Olivia turned, her face a picture of rapture. "Nathaniel, look! It's a shower of falling stars. Look, Eloise!"

Nathaniel handed the baby to Olivia, watching as Eloise stopped crying and looked with rapture at the stars.

"Ungrateful child. I'm the one

who built this tower."

Olivia laughed. "She'll thank you when she's older." She reached up and kissed him passionately. "I'll thank you right now."

"You can thank me tonight."

"Nathaniel!"

He wrapped his arms around her, staring at the night sky. "I'm sorry the tower wasn't finished until after Eloise was born, Livvy." He squeezed her. "I was quite tired of sleeping outside in that chair."

Olivia smiled. "I couldn't have climbed the stairs anyway with that big belly."

They watched together until the shower of stars faded, until Eloise began crying again. Olivia and Nathaniel looked at each other and shared a moment of complete togetherness.

She said loudly over the wails, "Thank you for teaching me the acts of seduction, Mr. Jenkins. And the art of love."

Nathaniel kissed her tenderly,

also speaking loudly. "It was my pleasure, Mrs. Jenkins. Entirely my pleasure."

And they went downstairs, tossing ideas back and forth on how to silence the interminable screeching.

*　*　*

THE RELUCTANT BRIDE
COLLECTION

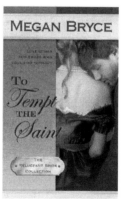

Available in ebook, paperback, and audio

www.meganbryce.com

A
TEMPORARY
ENGAGEMENT

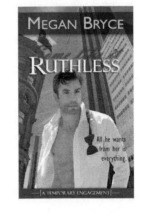

Available in ebook
and paperback

www.meganbryce.com

Printed in Great Britain
by Amazon